SO DARK A SHADOW

For three hundred years there have been D'alquens at Westings. Sir James intends that his line shall continue there in spite of modern taxation and the war that killed his sons. His daughter, Drusilla, agrees with him. This was her main motive in becoming engaged to her cousin, Julian, heir to the entailed estate. But a mysterious shadow spreads across life at Westings. Before it clears, murder is done, and all that Drusilla has cherished is threatened.

FREDA HURT

SO DARK
A SHADOW

Complete and Unabridged

LINFORD
Leicester

First published in Great Britain

First Linford Edition
published 1996

British Library CIP Data

Hurt, Freda
    So dark a shadow.—Large print ed.—
Linford mystery library
    1. English fiction—20th century
    I. Title
    823.9′14 [F]

    ISBN 0–7089–7935–1

Published by
F. A. Thorpe (Publishing) Ltd.
Anstey, Leicestershire

Set by Words & Graphics Ltd.
Anstey, Leicestershire
Printed and bound in Great Britain by
T. J. Press (Padstow) Ltd., Padstow, Cornwall

This book is printed on acid-free paper

1

I HAVE good reason to remember the day Alan Laird first came to Westings Court; a close grey morning, with the rooks' black wings flapping ponderously in a pewter-coloured sky, and the trees looking overburdened with foliage and standing so still and silent they seemed to be watching and waiting for something. But perhaps that particular fancy came to me because I myself was expecting the arrival of Dr. Robertson and I was feeling anxious and concerned about my father, who had been having some sort of heart attack for the third time in as many weeks.

Watching from the north window of the gallery, I heard a car approaching up the drive and knew at once that it wasn't the old doctor's sober Austin, which he had never been known to drive at a faster speed than thirty-five miles an hour, for birth, death, or a ruptured appendix, and which he slowed down to about ten once he had passed between the stone gateposts of Westings.

The grey two-seater that emerged from the screen of dark, heavy-leaved rhododendrons — now past their flowering — was going a good deal faster than that. The top was down and the driver and solitary occupant was a black-haired young man, a stranger. I saw him turn his head briefly to glance at the great cedar that cast so dark a shadow not even grass seemed able to flourish where it lay. A magnificent giant of a tree, said to be over two centuries old, there had always seemed something sinister to me in its beauty, since I had heard of the part it had played in a certain grim story.

Then, as the young man lifted his eyes to the house, with the look of somebody seeing its old rosy grace for the first time, I drew back a little, not wishing to be caught staring. I heard the car sweep round to the gravelled terrace in front of the house and stop.

I walked along the gallery, past the portraits that since my early childhood had seemed to watch me. I had always had the fancy that the painted eyes of the D'alquen women, in particular, were aware of me, the latest female of the family. The first of them, Drusilla Harcourt, who had married Jan D'alquen when he arrived from Holland in Dutch William's train, I had been named after and was said to resemble. It's true that we both had brown eyes in contrast to hair of an almost silvery fairness. But the hair of my ancestress, in the picture, was all delicate ringlets, while mine was thick and straight. Her mouth was smaller than mine, and her nose had a more chiselled elegance. The pale oval of her face was set on a voluptuously full white throat. There was certainly none of that alluring plumpness about me. I had been a skinny child, tall beyond my years, and was at twenty-one a slender five feet seven.

I reached the top of the broad oak staircase just as Friedrich, our butler and general factotum, limped across the hall to the main door. I called down to him softly.

"We can't receive visitors now, Friedrich."

I could see the bald yellowish scalp between the grey strands of his hair. Then he looked up at me and bowed silently, in a manner that was still rather foreign in spite of all the years he had lived in England.

I remained where I was while he opened the door, faintly curious in the midst of my anxiety. Once I turned away, fancying I had heard a sound from my father's room. But it was nothing. When I looked down again Friedrich was crossing the hall in the direction of the staircase, escorting the young man, who was carrying a small case. The stranger was tall, and made our Austrian servant look frailer than ever.

I gave an exclamation and began descending the stairs. Both men looked up. The young man with a startled air at first and then with an intent stare. He had brilliant blue eyes set in a rather craggy face. He must have used a pocket-comb while he waited in the porch, for his dark hair, that had been blown about in the open car in spite of the windless weather, was now in order. Then I saw that he had lowered his gaze and his face wore a stern and unsmiling expression.

"This is Dr. Laird, Miss Silla," Friedrich was saying. "Dr. Robertson is not to be found."

"Miss D'alquen?" said the young man abruptly, glancing up again from under his lowered brows. "I'm Dr. Robertson's new assistant, Alan Laird. What's the trouble?"

"My father has had another heart attack," I said. "But he seems slightly better now. It's always the way, isn't

5

it, when the doctor comes?"

I was wondering if his manner meant that he was feeling shy at being called to the manor in this way.

Westings Court is not one of the great houses of England, but it has beauty and distinction. Built towards the end of the seventeenth century, it has been occupied by my family for close on three hundred years, and for all that time the D'alquens have been of considerable importance in the county. My father, too, was a man of some attainment, having had a fairly well known parliamentary career till illness cut it short before he could reach real eminence.

"I'll see him at once," said Dr. Laird bluntly.

He took the hand I had stretched out to him, held it for the merest moment and released it quickly.

"Which way?" he snapped.

I gestured up the stairs and he went past me without ceremony. I caught Friedrich's eye and he gave the slightest of shrugs and turned down his mouth at the corners. Having been in my father's employment for longer than I could remember, he was privileged and knew it.

My father still slept in the ante-room leading out of the big main bedroom, left exactly as it was when my mother had died there six years earlier and never used. That wasn't the only part of the house shut up and in disuse. The drawing-room, with its console tables, tapestried chairs and one or two valuable pictures, and the big dining-room were both kept shrouded and locked. We lived very quietly at Westings and entertained little.

Leading the way into my father's room, I saw the scene for a moment as it might strike a stranger and thought what a foil for each other the two occupants were. It was a small but charming room, high-ceilinged and long windowed, with an old wallpaper patterned with small exotic birds. There was a great tallboy against one wall. My father looked a frail figure in the narrow bed, propped up with pillows. He had a slightly birdlike appearance himself, with his crest of white hair, handsome hawk nose and dark eyes. Overflowing the chair beside the bed was the fat old woman, with her small smudged features, creased eyes and dried looking red-brown wig.

Nanny Price had looked much as she did now from my earliest memory of her. She had been elderly then and was quite old now, though active in spite of her size. She had never been my nurse, having been promoted to housekeeper when my two half-brothers had grown beyond her care, which was years before I was born. But she had been 'Nanny' to two generations, and was still called so by members of the family. She always wore black, setting off her enormous brooches, which still looked absurdly small by contrast with her vast bosom.

My father turned his head on the supporting pillows as we entered and I was relieved to see that his colour was still improving and that his breathing was less laboured.

"This is Dr. Laird, Daddy," I said. "Dr. Robbie has been called away."

"Good of you to come, Dr. Laird," said my father, with a faint gasp, extending his thin white hand.

He glanced at me as Nanny rose ponderously from her chair and I smiled at him as serenely as I could and went out. I knew how he hated me to see him laid low.

I waited downstairs in the hall, which we used as a sitting-room. It was of a considerable size and given importance by two stately pillars. In fact the Chesterfield and great armchairs, set about the Chinese carpet spread before the wide fireplace, looked insignificant there. But there were fine views from the tall windows and in the summer it was a very pleasant place.

The dogs had been let in while I was upstairs, and Rollo, the old retriever, came and laid his chin on my knees, knowing that something was wrong, while Davis, the corgi, watched the stairs expectantly.

It was quite a long time before I heard feet coming down them and I had a feeling of anxiety and even fear by then. Heart trouble in a person dear to one can be a terrifying thing, and though old Dr. Robertson had pronounced my father's first attack as no more than palpitations brought on by exertion and a stomach upset, he had seemed faintly disturbed and puzzled by the subsequent attacks, which had taken a rather different form. He had even suggested that my father should see a specialist if the symptoms occurred again.

There had been movements upstairs while I waited. Doors opening and shutting and the rather thumping steps of Nanny going to and fro.

When Alan Laird at last came down I rose and went to meet him impatiently.

"Well? How is he?" I asked quickly.

He stood with the dogs sniffing round his feet and looked at me strangely. Instead of answering my question he said harshly: "Have you left the nursing of Sir James entirely to that old woman?"

I was surprised and nettled by his tone, but I answered calmly: "Yes. He prefers it. Mrs. Price is very experienced for one thing, and I'm not."

"And no doubt you thoroughly approve of this very experienced person dosing him with her own concoctions," he said in sarcastic tones and with an accent more markedly Scottish than ever.

"What?" I cried. I was puzzled by his obvious anger, annoyed too, but I tried to speak patiently.

"I know Nanny is a great believer in simple country remedies," I said. "But there's no harm in that, surely."

"Simple country remedies!" he exploded. "She's been poisoning the man with digitalis."

Shocked, but not really convinced, I frowned at him.

"But she wouldn't!" I exclaimed.

"Oh, I'm not saying it was deliberate," he admitted. "But it's my opinion Sir James's symptoms — weak pulse, slowing down and coupling of the heart beats in particular — are entirely consistent with digitalis poisoning. And there's a glass by his bedside that certainly never contained the medicine Dr. Robertson prescribed.

"Has Nanny admitted giving him digitalis?" I asked, now greatly disturbed.

"No," he said, frowning. "And Sir James hedged, when I questioned him. But I saw the look he gave her and I wasn't fooled by her talk of herb-tea. An infusion of foxglove leaves was what she meant."

I understood my father's loyalty to an old servant, but for me his health and safety came first.

"I did see her, the other day, coming back to the house with a bunch of foxgloves," I said. "But are you sure you're not mistaken? Dr. Robertson said nothing about poisoning when he saw my father during his last attack which was very like this one."

"It's very likely the suspicion would never have occurred to him," said the young man stiffly. "Mind, I'm not saying that Dr. Robertson isn't a very good doctor. But I've brought an entirely fresh mind to the case — fresh and unprejudiced."

"Unprejudiced?" I repeated.

His bright blue eyes stared into mine. The level of them was quite a bit higher than my own and that put me at a slight disadvantage.

"I mean I'm not an old friend of the family, Miss D'alquen," he said. "And Westings Court and its traditions — all very fine no doubt — mean nothing to me."

"I see," I said. I resented what I took to be a sneer at my father and me and our beloved home and his implication that Dr. Robbie was something of a snob. Then concern for my father swept aside all other feeling.

"But what's to be done? Is my father seriously ill?" I asked anxiously.

"He won't die of it?" he answered. "I've taken the simple steps immediately available for counteracting the poison — and made your overweight Mrs. Price run about a bit in the process. I think it was probably only a mild dose of digitalis she gave Sir James, but that the patient has an intolerance to the drug." Then, with a return of his aggressive manner he added: "You'd certainly better see it doesn't happen again, however."

"Of course," I said rather haughtily.

"Maybe you're over young for the responsibility," he told me, looking down his nose. "But I understand you're Sir James's next of kin."

"Maybe you're over young yourself, Dr. Laird," I snapped, losing patience with him.

He flushed. "If you're not satisfied with my professional services — " he began.

"Oh don't be so pompous!" I cried. Then I gave a laugh at his surprised and offended expression. "I'm sorry," I said. "But you don't seem to realise how upsetting your revelation has been. And you haven't been exactly sympathetic."

His manner became slightly more friendly. "It seemed to me a matter for straight talking," he said. "But I apologise if I have been too abrupt."

"Thank you," I said. "Well, I am Sir James's next of kin, as you put it. My mother died six years ago, and I have no brothers or sisters. My father had two sons by his first marriage, but they were both killed during the war, one in the army and one in the air force — both younger than I am now."

Of course I didn't tell him what I had learned as a child, that my father, a widower, had then married my quiet and unassuming mother mainly to provide new heirs for Westings. He had been disappointed when a girl was born, for title and estate were both tied to the male line of descent. I had grown to sympathise with his feelings, knowing that he cared for me deeply in spite of everything and had come to love my mother. Besides, I too was devoted to Westings and was myself prepared to marry for the sake of it, and to atone a little for being the wrong sex and the only child. Not that I wasn't very fond of my cousin Julian and pleased with my as yet unofficial engagement to him for other reasons. But married to him I should keep both the family name and the family home, and my sons — I felt sure we should have son — would ensure that my father's direct descendants would inherit Westings after all.

I said, as I walked with Alan to the door: "There's supposed to be a curse on the eldest sons of this house, you know."

Of course I didn't believe it, but the idea coming on top of my previous thoughts made me shiver secretly.

He nodded. "I was told some such

old wives' tale," he said.

I went out into the porch with him and he glanced towards the great cedar, which could be glimpsed from there.

"That's a fine big tree," he remarked.

"Oh yes, and we've a ghost in connection with that," I said. "A servant who committed suicide by hanging himself from it fifty years ago. I believe the curse has got something to do with him. He fancied himself wronged by the family in some way." I smiled. "But I don't suppose you believe in the ghost any more than the curse."

He grinned at me, suddenly looking young and vulnerable. "I don't believe in it at this moment," he replied. "But if you were to ask me the same question passing your great cedar on a dark night I might give a different answer. I haven't Highland blood for nothing."

He was becoming more and more human and I was liking him better and better.

"I've not seen poor Will Price myself," I said. "But he's supposed to have been seen from time to time by various people — Nanny herself for one."

"Price?" he said quickly. "The same name as your Nanny!"

"He was her husband," I explained. "Poor woman! She lost her son too. But that was later, and he didn't die, just ran away from home. It was all a long time ago."

"It would be," he said.

I think we both shared at that moment a feeling of joy that we were young and had our lives before us. Perhaps there was more than that to it, even then, the something that was between us.

As if to break the link, he looked past me into the hall, then stood back and gazed up at the beautifully proportioned front of the house.

"It's a fine place!" he murmured. Then, darting that brilliant blue glance at me again, he added: "But aren't you

18

bored here, with no work to do?"

I looked at him in astonishment. "But I've plenty," I cried. "Didn't I tell you? I've been mistress here since I was sixteen."

"I meant *real* work," he said bluntly. "You've servants, haven't you? Even a housekeeper, if that's what that old Price woman is."

Then, reading my annoyance in my face, he said, with all his stiffness back. "But it's no business of mine. I'll say good morning to you, Miss D'alquen. No doubt Dr. Robertson will be calling to see your father as soon as he can."

"I hope so," I said coldly.

When I had closed the door and gone into the hall again I relieved my feelings a little by saying aloud: "Of all the arrogant, self-righteous prigs!" Then I flew upstairs to my father.

Nanny had left him for a moment and he was lying back against the pillows looking pale and weary. But he opened his eyes and smiled at me.

"Daddy!" I said, taking his hand and

holding it in both mine. "Are you all right?"

"Yes, of course, darling," he answered. "I hope that rather brash young man hasn't been frightening you." He gave a chuckle. "What a bedside manner!"

"A ghastly young man!" I said violently.

"But a damn sight more efficient than old Robbie, apparently," said my father. "To tell you the truth, I rather like the lad."

"But you don't think he was right, do you?" I cried anxiously.

"Yes. If you mean do I think Nanny has been poisoning me," he said. He chuckled again. "With the best intentions, of course. But that's the way Hell's paved, or so it has been said."

I clasped his hand closer. "Promise me you'll never never take any more of Nanny's medicines," I pleaded.

"Don't worry, darling. I forswear them from this moment," he said gaily. "That young man put the fear of God into me as well as into Nanny."

She came billowing in at that point. "My medicines never did a mite of harm to a living soul, Sir James," she pronounced dramatically. "But faith's worth more than potions, and trusts the half of healing."

She was always full of these Sybil-like sayings.

"If you take the word of a stranger that's not much more than a boy and no gentleman though he may be a doctor, then there's little good I can do you," she declared with great dignity.

"Or harm either," said my father, with a little grimace at me.

"It's that young man that's done the poisoning," said Nanny darkly. "He's poisoned your mind against me, Sir James."

"Oh nonsense, Nanny!" said my father impatiently. "We all know you meant well. And I won't have you abusing Dr. Laird. Now let's hear no more about it."

But I couldn't help thinking about it

a good deal and wondering what would have happened if Nanny had gone on giving him digitalis and Dr. Robertson hadn't discovered it. And that evening, as I put on the sapphire ring Julian had given me and which I wore only privately as yet, I found myself thinking about the blueness of Alan Laird's eyes instead of my cousin and fiancé.

2

THE next day Dr. Robertson came. The weather had turned warm and sunny and we were sitting out on the terrace, my father and I. He still had an invalidish air, but had insisted on getting up, and now sat leaning back against the cushions with a rug handy for his knees.

The old doctor's ruddy face was smiling gently as he came towards us, having parked his car on the wide gravelled space in front of the house, where, in the old days, a coach and horses had had room to turn. But as he drew near I saw that his eyes were not smiling. Wrinkled as they were against the sunshine, there was a lot of anxiety in them.

"Well, James?" he said, when he had greeted me with a playful bow. "What's this I hear about your dosing yourself with digitalis?"

He and my father were old friends, though he was the elder of the two by several years.

"My dear Robbie, your young man must have told you it was Nanny Price who was doing the dosing," said my father. "And I wasn't to know the poor old fool was poisoning me. You've said yourself that her concoctions could do no harm and might even do some good."

"I was talking about her elder-flower lotion and herb tea," said the doctor. "Not an infusion of foxgloves. She seems to have grown ambitious in her old age."

"Are you sure Dr. Laird wasn't mistaken?" I asked. "Nanny has never actually admitted the infusion of fox-gloves."

"There's no doubt about it, though," said Dr. Robbie. "Dr. Laird brought back a sample he collected from the glass so rashly left by the bedside and had it analysed."

"Nanny should have destroyed the evidence," remarked my father with a chuckle.

"Aren't you both taking this too lightly?" I burst out.

But at that moment Friedrich came towards us carrying a chair for the doctor, who greeted him kindly and enquired about his rheumatism.

"Better, Doctor, better thank you," replied Friedrich, with his little bow. Then, sinking his voice to a pleading murmur, he said: "May I speak to you privately before you go, sir?"

"Surely, surely," said the old doctor quietly. He looked thoughtfully after the retreating Austrian then turned to me.

"What were you saying, Silla? That we're treating this digitalis business too lightly? I'm not really, my dear. I mean to talk to Mrs. Price very severely."

"She'll take it from you, Robbie," said my father. "Your forthright young man offended her deeply. He didn't mince his words with me, either."

The doctor chuckled. "Alan Laird is scarcely a social paragon," he admitted. "But he's a good doctor, and he'll learn. He's been a great help to me already. It's one of life's little ironies that the practice has increased with the development of the new estate at Windham, just as I've got too old to cope."

"I don't wish to take the bread out of your mouth — or is it cake now?" said my father. "But I'd like to see the new housing estate at Windham transfered to the moon." And he gave an imperious wave of the hand.

"Oh come! People have got to live somewhere," Dr. Robbie expostulated.

"Quite. But I'd rather they didn't do it on my doorstep," said my father, with an arrogance that was unconscious.

"Windham is two miles from here, as the crow flies," said the doctor. "Some doorstep!"

"You were talking about Dr. Laird," I reminded him.

"So I was. Angus Duncan, the heart

specialist recommended him to me, you know. Laird's a kind of prodigy of his. I told you at the time, didn't I, James?"

"So you did," said my father. "But what's his background?"

"He's a child of the manse," said Dr. Robbie. "and shared his particular one with five siblings. I believe the family was as poor as the proverbial church mouse — kirk mouse, I should say, in this case." He smiled, pleased with his own wit. "He tells me his grandparents were crofters, in Glenairlie. Isn't that where your grandparents had a country house, James? At Glenairlie in Argyllshire?"

"Yes," said my father. "I used to go there as a boy. Quite a coincidence! Laird could have had a worse background."

"Much worse," agreed the doctor. "But it has given him a sense of life being indeed real and earnest. The lad doesn't know how to play or take things lightly."

"I had an idea he didn't think much

of me," I said, and smiled to show them how lightly I was taking that. "He obviously thought I ought to be out fighting my way in the world, serving the community by emptying bedpans or at least pounding a typewriter."

The two elderly men turned to look at me and a similar expression of affectionate admiration came into their eyes. "What nonsense!" said my father.

"You're like a jewel in the right setting here at Westings," said the old doctor. He belonged to a generation that could still say pretty things.

I belonged to a generation that had lost the art of receiving such compliments. "You're both too kind to me, I'm afraid," I said.

"You belong here," said my father firmly. "And, now that you are to marry Julian, I hope that will be true for the rest of your life."

"I don't know how I've managed to keep the great news to myself, but I have," said the old doctor, smiling at me. "I suppose there'll be a formal announcement as soon as your nephew comes back from America, James."

"Yes," said my father. "It will be a great occasion at Westings."

If only he had known how much was to happen before that day.

"Julian and his mother hold most of the shares in Jobson's Jams and Jellies," continued my father. "Her father was old George Jobson, you know. With his money, Silla and her husband will be able to carry on at Westings without opening it to the mob. Even with my death duties paid up, I'm sure I would come back and haunt the place if it was desecrated by screaming brats and transistors and ice cream cartons and orange peel."

"I doubt if this would attract that kind of visitor," remarked the doctor. "Westings is no Woburn, you know."

"No, thank God," said my father. "Westings is for the connoisseur, if it's for anybody outside the family."

Soon after that Dr. Robbie took his leave of us and went into the house in search of Friedrich.

"I wonder what Friedrich wants to see him for," remarked my father. "He said his rheumatism was better. I hope there's nothing seriously wrong with the poor chap." He had never ceased to feel sympathy for our Austrian servant since he had known that Friedrich had suffered the agonies of a concentration camp for some trivial offence against the Nazis.

"I've often wondered that the ordeal didn't affect his mind," my father added.

But it was not any trouble with his own mind that was worrying Friedrich, as I was to find out.

Later that day the old doctor rang up. "I've been thinking, since I saw you this morning, that it's a long time since you came to tea, my dear," he said, when he had enquired about my father's progress. "Now that I have an assistant I'm free in the afternoons more often. Could you bear to come and keep an old dodderer company

30

tomorrow, and chat over a cup of tea? Mrs. Budge went rushing off to the kitchen to look in her recipe-book at the mere suggestion you might. I can promise you the results of a great bake, if that's anything."

"I don't need any inducement, you modest man," I said. "Of course I'll come with pleasure, for your company alone. But I'm not saying I won't make a pig of myself over those delicious cakes and scones your housekeeper makes."

I answered gaily, but I was worried. I had sensed at once that something more important than a mere invitation to tea lay behind the old doctor's request. My fear was that he wished to talk to me about my father's health where there was no danger of the patient overhearing, which meant there must be something seriously wrong.

There was nothing antique and precious about Woodside, Dr. Robertson's house. It was simply pleasantly old-fashioned, with its rose-covered porch and neat double-frontage. When I was a child I had often been to tea with Mrs. Robertson, a gentle soul with a strong sense of humour, who had loved children but then childless herself. Now Dr. Robbie was a widower, looked after by the widowed Mrs. Budge, who was really rather a treasure. Not only was she a wonderful cook, within the limitations of English dishes, she was clean and efficient and so fascinated by fractures, dislocations, strokes, operations and fevers it was clear she would never be able to tear herself away from a household where she got much of such things for such ordinary considerations as less work and more pay.

Dr. Robbie was cutting dead roses from the bushes in the oval bed in front of the house when I drove my small car in through the hospitably open gates that afternoon. He turned and showed such a smiling face when he heard me that I was rather reassured. Surely, I thought, my father's friend would never look so cheerful if my suspicions were right. I parked carefully, where the car would not block the drive — a necessary consideration here — and got out.

"What a pleasure to see you, my dear," said the doctor. "Let me give you a rose."

He cut a gorgeous Queen Elizabeth rose, not yet fully out, and I sniffed it and stuck it in the neck of my linen dress.

"Ah! Roses don't smell as they used to when I was young," he said, leading the way into the house.

The sitting-room hadn't really changed since I was a little girl. There were the same rugs on the polished parquet flooring, the same deep chairs and broad sofa, covered with a very similar cretonne. There were some old ivory chessmen set out on a board upon a little table in the window, as if in the middle of a game. Was Alan Laird, Dr. Robbie's opponent? Or had the vicar been called away in the midst of play?

I wondered if I should see anything of Alan. I wanted to ask casually if he was in, but found myself curiously unable to do so. It was as if, I thought uneasily, his comings and goings were of importance to me.

Then Mrs. Budge came in, wheeling the tea-trolley. She was a small sallow woman with prominent eyes and an eager manner. I greeted her and exclaimed at the home-baked scones and the walnut cake, the dishes of jam and the puffy sponge-sandwich, as in duty bound, but with a touch of genuine appreciation too.

"How fat I should get, if I came to tea here often," I remarked, smiling.

"Not you, Miss D'alquen," said Mrs. Budge, in a kind of glow of excited hospitality. "When you're young you need the nourishment. Young people's strength has to be built up. That's what I tell Dr. Laird, and he's eating a lot better than when he first came. Oh, a lot better. Not quite such skin and bone, poor young man! But, as Dr.

Robertson knows well, these things take time."

"Thank you, Mrs. Budge. Thank you," said Dr. Robbie quickly, and giving her a sharp glance — almost an angry glance, it seemed to me.

In fact, I got the impression he was afraid his housekeeper was going to say something indiscreet. Mrs. Budge certainly looked a little hurt and startled. Did she perhaps look a little guilty, too? I smiled at her warmly to make up for the doctor's brusqueness and she went out apparently quite happy again.

Dr. Robbie lifted the silver teapot. "Bless me! I haven't seen this since Winifred died," he said. "You're honoured, my dear."

"I feel it," I assured him. "And what a spread!"

"We must try to do justice to it, or Mrs. Budge's feelings may be hurt," he told me.

"I don't need persuading. I eat like a hungry hunter, you know," I said.

"And stay so slim!" sighed the doctor, glancing down at his comfortable paunch. "Ah me! I can remember when I ate like a horse, too, and thought ten stone a great weight to be. But I played football in those days, and boxed. Now I play golf — when I have time. Not that golf isn't a good healthy means of exercise. Your father ought to take it up again."

I took a golden brown scone from the plate he offered me, then looked him straight in the eyes. "Dr. Robbie, please tell me truthfully, how *is* my father?" I asked.

"Why, there's nothing seriously wrong with him, to my mind," answered the old doctor, to my immense relief. "Though, as you know, I did suggest his having a second opinion. I was a little puzzled before by symptoms that seemed not to apply. But, as you know, my assistant discovered the cause of them. Stupid of me not to have suspected digitalis poisoning, but, frankly, it never occurred to me."

"Why should it have done," I said heartily, for I was fond of the old man. "Of course, Nanny should never have interfered, and Daddy shouldn't have encouraged her."

The doctor put down his cup and looked at me with an expression in his eyes that told me he was coming to the real reason of this little tea-party.

"Drusilla," he said. "You know Friedrich wanted a private word with me yesterday when I visited your father? Well, it was not about himself he wished to consult me, but about Nanny Price."

"But Nanny seems quite well!" I explained. "I know she's old and awfully fat, but she seems as fit and strong as ever."

"It's not her physical fitness Friedrich is concerned about, but her mental state," said Dr. Robbie. "He seems to think her mind is going."

"You mean she's becoming senile?" I said anxiously.

"It's possible," said the doctor.

"Deterioration of the brain sets in with different people at different ages. With many it never seems to show itself at all. But with the thickening of the arteries the flow of blood to the brain becomes restricted and it doesn't get its proper nourishment, and so is unable to work efficiently."

"But she hasn't seemed any different to me," I cried. "What makes Friedrich think she is breaking up?"

"He says he found her manner very strange one morning when he took her breakfast-tray up to her room, as she hadn't come down at the usual time. She babbled about having seen the ghost of her husband, William Price, and talked about his wanting revenge," said the doctor.

In spite of the pleasant sunny room, I felt a little shiver run down my spine.

"But if she had overslept and had a bad dream, she might not have been fully awake when she spoke to Friedrich," I said.

Dr. Robbie nodded. "Apparently

Friedrich suggested that to her and she became quite angry, saying that she knew when she was awake and when she wasn't and Friedrich was a fool."

I stirred my tea and avoided looking at the doctor as I said: "I suppose you don't think she could have seen — well what she said she did?"

I half-expected him to laugh. But he didn't.

"I've lived nearly three quarters of a century now, Silla," he said, "and in that time I've come across one or two happenings that can't be explained in the light of our present knowledge, and heard of quite a few more. Extra Sensory Perception is a fine term given nowadays by a lot of clever men to something they don't understand but have come to believe exists. And who am I to say they are wrong? At the same time, I think it's far more probable that Mrs. Price is becoming senile than that the ghost of her husband has appeared again, after he has been dead fifty years, demanding vengeance."

I had forgotten to eat in my interest, and he passed the plate of scones to me again, with a dish of raspberry jam, reminding me of our duty to his housekeeper.

"But vengeance for what?" I asked, as I helped myself to the jam. "I've never really known what the grudge was that William Price was supposed to have had against the family, I know he was one of the grooms, and that Nanny is said to have married beneath her when she chose him. I imagine she was terribly in love with him — though that's hard to grasp now."

Thinking of the fat, rather dull old woman, it did indeed seem difficult to credit that she was ever a slave to passion.

"*He* was terribly in love with *her*, according to what I've been told by ancient gossips," said the doctor. "And I've no doubt she had some sort of fancy for him in the beginning. She must have done, to have married him.

Apparently she was a very pretty girl, though her chances of making a really good match can't have been very great down here. You know, when I first came here thirty-five years ago, she was still a fine looking woman. A considerable armful, mind you, but nothing like she is now."

"Well?" I said, as he took a mouthful of scone and made a rather long pause.

He glanced rather strangely at me. "I doubt if I ought to be talking to you like this," he said. "I know what a strong sense of loyalty your father has, towards his family as well as to those who have served it as long and faithfully as Mrs. Price has. He doesn't like any mention of the matter and has always scotched all rumours of it. If he had wanted you to know anything about it — "

"I'm a big girl now, Dr. Robbie," I interrupted him, smiling. "And if it concerns my family, surely I've a right to know what has been said, whether it's true or not."

"As to the truth of it, who am I to say?" said the doctor. "And it all happened a long time ago. It's the fact of Nanny Price still being alive and a member of the household at Westings that makes it a delicate matter. You see, the story is that William killed himself because he discovered his wife had been deceiving him for years. She had had a lover."

"But surely the more usual thing is to kill the lover — or the wife!" I said.

"In this case the lover was already dead. He was your grandfather's elder brother."

"My grandfather's elder brother?" I repeated. "You must mean my Great Uncle Charles. He was a gay bachelor and got himself killed in a hunting accident."

Doctor Robbie nodded and began carefully cutting into the walnut cake, rather as though he were performing a surgical operation.

"I've always believed that was what gave rise to the legend of the curse upon the eldest son," he said. "And of course the loss of your two half-brothers gave the story new life."

"Possibly," I said, and added thoughtfully: "William Price must have been a very sensitive type to have committed suicide over an affair that was past and done with."

"If it was new to him, it could be that in losing his faith in his wife he lost it in everything else," said the old doctor. "But we've gone a long way from the point, haven't we. It's not William Price's mental state fifty years ago with which we're concerned, but his widow's mental state today. I mentioned what Friedrich had told me to Dr. Laird because he had seen the old lady quite recently. I asked him what he thought. He was non-committal, but he did suggest something that I felt I ought to pass on to you."

"Yes?" I said impatiently, as he paused to offer me the walnut cake.

His shrewd old eyes met mine. "Dr. Laird said that *if* it was true that

Mrs. Price was degenerating mentally, it was possible that her motive in dosing your father with digitalis was neither benevolent nor harmless," he told me.

I stared at him, with my hand still extended towards the cake. I wondered if I could have understood aright.

"You don't mean — you *can't* mean that Nanny might have poisoned Daddy deliberately!" I cried. Then I became indignant. "I think it was disgusting of Alan Laird to have made such a suggestion. What does *he* know about any of us? I'm surprised you should have considered it even worth passing on. Now, Dr. Robbie, confess that the idea would never have entered your head if that objectionable man hadn't put it there."

"No, it wouldn't," said the old doctor, calmly and quietly. "But remember, the notion that your father was taking digitalis at all never entered my head either. Do take some cake, my dear."

That brought me up short. I took

a slice automatically. "Maybe," I said reflectively. "But I know Nanny. I'm quite sure she meant no harm. Why, she's devoted to my father."

"Perhaps I should have cut the sandwich first," remarked the doctor. "What do you think?"

His manner was so normal and natural that it seemed absurd to think he was seriously considering the possibility of a would-be murderess loose at Westings.

I said the cake was very nice, or some such banality, and he immediately shot at me: "I suppose you're very fond of Mrs. Price."

This took me by surprise. Was I very fond of Nanny? I had never asked myself the question before. Now that I did I found the answer disquieting. No, I wasn't very fond of her. I merely accepted her. There were times, even, when I found her faintly repellent.

"Nanny has always been part of my home," I said firmly. "Of course I care about her."

"Spoken like your father's daughter," he said with a smile. "Well, I thought it best to warn you, though I'm not saying Mrs. Price isn't innocent as the driven snow and sane as a sanitary inspector."

We both laughed. But he added with a deep under-lying seriousness: "Don't take anything for granted, Drusilla. I knew it was no use saying anything to your father. He might have taken another dose from the old lady just to prove his faith in her good will."

"That's exactly what Daddy would have done," I admitted. "All right, Dr. Robbie, I'll try to keep an open mind and watch poor old Nanny as closely as possible."

"Good girl!" said the doctor, and immediately changed the subject and became just a kindly and charming old friend. Only as he said good-bye he remarked with a slight twinkle in his eyes: "So you think my assistant is an objectionable man."

"Yes, I do," I said, and heard a

little voice in my mind say distinctly: "Liar!"

"I thought you young people banded together against us old fogies nowadays," remarked the doctor.

I passed that off with a laugh, telling him I wouldn't allow him to call himself names. He was far from being an old fogie.

He stood waving as I drove off, and I caught a glimpse of Mrs. Budge, whom I had praised and thanked for her excellent baking, peeping round a curtain like an inquisitive mouse. There was a scent of stocks coming from the flower border. Dr. Robbie's white hair shone like candy floss in the late afternoon sunshine. It was a scene that, for various reasons, stayed in my mind for a long time.

The way back to Westings lay mainly along a narrow winding road sunk between banks where the soil had been washed away from the branching roots of great beeches, exposing their twisted shapes, often strangely beautiful. The trees made the lane a green tunnel in summer, but I knew it so well that its dangers to the motorist didn't worry me. I must confess, however, that my mind on this occasion wasn't entirely on my driving. I was thinking of old Nanny Price and the suspicion concerning her, which I had not really been able to dismiss. For one thing, I knew the old doctor was no scandalmonger. If he thought that there was a danger — even a remote one — that our housekeeper was mentally sick, then it must be considered.

I was wondering whether I could question Friedrich myself about her, or whether he might think Dr. Robbie had betrayed a confidence in passing on his fears to me, as I plunged into the leafy gloom of the lane. I had travelled only a little way along it when a klaxon sounded close behind me. By habit I was well over on to the left side of the road and going at a cautious pace, but I slowed up still more as a long, low, red shape shot by.

The fool! I thought. It only needs an oncoming car now —

And at that moment it happened. An open grey car appeared. I had a glimpse of Alan Laird's face behind the windscreen, wearing the expression of a man who sees a precipice open suddenly before him. Then the red car was right in front of me.

I braked violently, turned the steering—wheel so that I saw a tangle of tree-roots coming to meet me. Then cymbals clashed and great gongs sounded.

3

THERE were voices a long way off and, nearer to me, a rushing sound. Hammers beat soundlessly inside my head and dark veils moved in front of my eyes. The voices came closer, two voices speaking quietly, one feminine and the other masculine and faintly familiar.

"What a good thing her face wasn't touched," said the feminine voice. "She's quite beautiful, isn't she."

"You think so?" said the masculine voice.

"Yes. Don't you, Doctor?" the feminine voice sounded slightly amused and challenging.

"Yes. She's beautiful," said the other voice, with an oddly grudging note in it.

Who were they talking about? Perhaps if I opened my eyes I could see this beautiful person too. There were weights on my eyelids, but I managed to drag them up. Light stabbed my eyes like knives and I shut them again, groaning aloud.

"She's coming round, Doctor," said the feminine voice.

I made another effort and opened my eyes again. I saw the face of Alan Laird just above me. His brilliant blue eyes stared into mine. Things beyond came into focus. I could see a white wall and a window with drawn curtains. A wave of giddiness and nausea made my sight darken, and once more I groaned and closed my eyes.

"Just relax, Miss D'alquen," said Alan Laird gently. "Don't worry. You'll soon be feeling much better."

"What happened?" I asked feebly, with a confused memory of having been driving somewhere.

"You've been involved in a car accident. But there's no great harm done," said the doctor, reassuringly.

My father was wrong, I thought. His

bedside manner was wonderful. The meaning of the scrap of conversation I had just overheard suddenly came to me.

"I'm glad you think I'm beautiful," I said, and heard a sound like a smothered giggle. I opened my eyes and glimpsed the craggy young face frowning and the blue eyes wary and strangely hurt looking.

"She's wandering again," I heard Alan Laird say. Then I sank back into darkness.

Somebody had said I was in an accident. But this was absurd. What was wrong was that Nanny had poisoned Mrs. Budge's walnut cake, and I had eaten a slice. I must warn Dr. Robbie not to let my father have any.

I struggled to open my eyes and sit up. This time the light was subdued and the pain to my eyes was negligible, but my head ached abominably.

"My father!" I gasped. "He must be told."

I glimpsed a round white arm, a

snowy cuff and a blue and white striped sleeve and a hand pushed me gently but firmly back.

"Don't worry, Miss D'alquen," said the feminine voice I had heard before. "Sir James has been told. He was here earlier, but you were asleep. He asked me to give you his dear love as soon as you woke up and to say that he is coming to see you in the morning."

I could see her clearly now, a pretty dark-haired nurse with a face like a sophisticated kitten. I looked round me. I was in a small, clean, light room. I was in bed and wearing a nightdress that was not my own.

"Am I in hospital?" I said wonderingly.

"Yes. You had a bit of an accident," the nurse told me. "You bumped your head rather hard."

My memory was returning. "I remember I was driving along Jackdaw Lane and a car overtook me," I said. "Was Dr. Laird there?" I frowned, wondering if I had dreamed that bit.

"Yes," said the nurse, her pert face

suddenly sober. "He seems to have had a narrow squeak, too. The driver of that overtaking car must have been quite mad. *He's* not hurt at all."

"Dr. Laird isn't, is he. I thought he was here, earlier," I said quickly.

She gave me a curious look. "Yes Dr. Laird was here. You're the only one that got hurt," she said. "Your car's a bit damaged, too. Fortunately it tipped up when it hit a tree, mounted the bank, or outspread roots or something, and you shot up and hit the roof, instead of being sent forward into the windscreen and the steering column." She began to tuck in my bedclothes.

"I'll get you a drink, then you can go to sleep again," she said.

"What time is it?" I asked, still very confused.

"Five past three — in the morning."

I had my drink and went to sleep again. There seemed nothing else to do and the desire to sleep was compulsive.

When I finally woke it was broad daylight and Alan Laird was in the room again. He was holding my wrist lightly with his fingers on my pulse, and his eyes were thoughtful and abstracted looking.

Then he released my wrist and smiled at me. "Hullo," he said. "You're doing fine."

I was feeling much better, though my head was still aching. I put my hand up to it.

"Ah, you've got a bit of a bump there," he said. "But that will soon go down."

His face changed as if a cloud had passed over it. His rather deep-set eyes seemed to glower at me out of small caverns.

"It's no thanks to that friend of yours in the red car."

"My friend?" I repeated. "Do you mean that the driver who caused the accident was somebody I know?"

"He was on his way to Westings, or so he said," answered Alan. "His name is Adrian Price." He added grimly, "I made sure he told me the truth about that because I'm seeing to it that he gets charged with dangerous driving."

I started to shake my head, then thought better of it as a dull pain started up there.

"The only Price I know is Nanny," I said, and the memory of what Dr. Robbie and I had discussed concerning her suddenly hit me. I sat up.

"I must go home. I can't stay here," I said urgently.

"Nonsense! Of course you're staying here," said Alan in authoritative tones. "You're in no fit state to be out yet."

His eyes met mine. "You've no need to be worrying about your father," he added more gently. "Don't you remember that he's coming to see you this morning? And here's Sister anxious to get you washed and tidied in time for Matron's visit first."

Somebody called the quiet, sandy-haired Sister Jenkins at this point, and she went out with a smile and a murmured apology.

"You know why I'm worried," I

said accusingly. "It's about Nanny. According to you, she could be planning to poison my father again."

"Isn't Sir James a man of his word then?" he snapped.

"Of course he is. Absolutely," I answered indignantly.

"Then you've nothing to worry about, have you?" he said. "Especially if he's a man of sense, too, which I'm not so sure about, bearing all things in mind." He looked down his nose.

I controlled my anger and said with deliberate coldness: "He's more than a man of sense, Dr. Laird. He's a man of intellect, as well as of tact and kindness. But you wouldn't understand that."

We glowered at each other, then Sister Jenkins came forward, from the doorway.

"You mustn't excite yourself, dear," she told me. "Dr. Laird, we've quite a few more patients to see."

"I've no doubt," said Alan, making the final word sound almost like 'doot'. He stalked to the door. "Good morning, Miss D'alquen," he said stiffly.

"Good morning, Dr. Laird," I said with hauteur, and added after the door had closed on them: "Arrogant ass!" Then I leaned back against my pillows with my head throbbing but feeling alert and alive again. How that man got under my skin, I thought. And I under his, apparently. But he had agreed that I was beautiful. That gave me an absurd pang of pleasure, as if it was the first time ever that such a compliment had been paid me.

When I had been breakfasted and washed and tidied, and smiled upon by Matron, my father came, looking as always calm and immaculate, but with deep love and concern in his fine eyes.

"Daddy! You're all right?" I said anxiously.

He stooped and kissed me, then stood back with a laugh. "Am *I* all right? Darling! It's you who are the patient now," he said. "They tell me you had a little argument with a tree, through that damned young man overtaking in Jackdaw Lane and meeting young Laird almost head-on."

"I think I've had concussion," I said. "It felt most odd, when I could feel anything. But nothing very terrible is wrong with me."

"Thank God!" said my father.

"Dr. Laird says the young man was on his way to Westings. Do you know who he is, Daddy?" I said curiously.

"Yes. Something rather extraordinary has happened," answered my father. "You remember, of course, that Nanny had an only son, who ran away from home as a youth. Why, it must be over forty years ago! Well, this young man is his son, and he's brought his sister with him to look Nanny up." He added dryly: "Considering the manner of their arrival I must say I wish they had kept away."

But I was lost in wonder and wanted to ask all sorts of questions.

"Why did they wait all this time?" was the first one.

"Oh, apparently they have only quite recently discovered their grandmother's existence," said my father. "Their father is dead."

"What are they like?" I asked.

"Well, the boy has plenty of charm," said my father. "He's an actor. They're both on the stage, it seems. The sister is remarkably pretty."

"I think Miss D'alquen has talked long enough, Sir James," said Sister Jenkins, coming in before I had half done with the subject. "She still needs rest."

"Of course," said my father, rising instantly. "Goodbye, darling." He kissed my forehead.

"Good-bye, Daddy. And remember — no potions," I whispered.

"Not a thimbleful," he said reassuringly, smiling.

Later a nurse brought in an armful of hot-house flowers from Westings, with some of my own pretty nightdresses and bed-jackets. With the latter was a note from Nanny Price.

"Dear Miss Silla," she had written. "I'm that sorry it was my own grandson caused the nasty accident to you, but hope you will soon be quite well again. Such a surprise! With me not even knowing I was a grandmother. It seems my boy died a short time ago, and their mother has been dead quite a while. They haven't got a proper home, and I've been thinking it would be nice if Sir James Would let them rent the lodge, it being empty now Benson has gone to live with his married daughter in the village. Of course they would be away a lot, being actors. Well, no more for now. With best wishes, Nanny."

I stared at the squat black letters, that were rather like Nanny's person, with mixed feelings, sympathy with the old woman's desire to have her newly discovered family near her, some curiosity and some lingering resentment towards the driver of the red car. I was relieved, too, that Nanny had expressed herself so normally. There was no sign of a decaying intelligence here.

Hers was not the only letter I received. There were quite a number of little notes expressing concern and sympathy from friends and acquaintances, as well as so many offerings of fruit and flowers that I had most of it distributed round the little cottage hospital. The most important of the letters was from Julian.

I had a queer feeling of guilt as I opened it. It was not entirely a love letter, being full of news about his doings in the States, where he had gone to visit the American branches of Judson's Jams and Jellies. But at the end he had written: "Are you missing me, darling? I hope so. I can't tell you how often that lovely little mug of yours comes between me and the heavily jowled face of some captain of industry, but I'm afraid it will be several more weeks before I can hold you in my arms again. Then I shall let the world know that you belong to me, me, me."

Julian was nice, I told myself. Julian really loved me. I was a very lucky girl. I vowed I would make him a good wife.

Dr. Robbie popped in to see me for a few minutes, and told me how lucky I was, too, but for having escaped death and being now in such good hands.

"They tell me Dr. Laird came charging in here, carrying you unconscious in his arms, like some film hero," he said.

"Everybody has been awfully kind," I murmured, to hide the absurd thrill that gave me.

Next morning I felt almost completely recovered, but was assured it would be a different matter when I was on my feet and walking about. Alan Laird confirmed this when he came to see me, and took my pulse with his grave abstracted manner.

"But you're better," he said, releasing my wrist. "You can get up for a while, and go home tomorrow if you want to."

I had been thinking of his carrying me into the hospital in his arms and I said softly: "Thank you for all you've done for me, Dr. Laird. I shan't forget it."

But he turned wooden immediately. "I've only done my job, Miss D'alquen," he said. It was like a slap in the face. Well, if he wanted it like that.

"Of course," I said. "But how well you do it!" I smiled at Sister Jenkins. "How well you all do it." I sounded, I knew, horribly patronising. "But I shall certainly go home tomorrow. I'm needed there now."

At this point Sister was called to the door for another of those whispered conferences, and Alan darted me a piercing look.

"It seems to me that Westings can get on very well without you, for a while," he said. "As I pointed out to you before, Miss D'alquen, you have servants to do the real work."

64

"So you did, Dr. Laird," I said, mocking him. "But do you know that in my grandmother's day, when Westings was properly run, there were ten indoor servants, counting two nursemaids. Outside, there were a chauffeur, a groom and six gardeners. *I* run Westings with old Nanny, Friedrich, and a succession of women from the village who come in for a few hours a day. One of them is a part-time cook. We have one gardener, who is an old man. Sometimes he has a schoolboy to help him. I look after my own horse."

He looked down his nose. "You've no need to tell me times have changed," he said. "It's I who have been trying to tell you that."

"You've made it clear that you dislike me, if that's what you mean," I said, staring at him.

I was rewarded by seeing him start and redden. He met my eyes with his direct blue gaze.

"No. That's not true. You can't think

it," he said quickly. Then he steadied. "I don't dislike you personally," he said deliberately. "Only what you stand for."

"And what's that?" I asked, with a smile that cost me considerable effort.

"A kind of privilege," he told me seriously. "You were born with a silver spoon in your mouth, and you're not even grateful. In fact, you're sorry for yourself because it wasn't a gold one."

"That's not true," I broke in angrily.

"Look at you now," he retorted. "Oh, you've had a bit of a bash and a shake-up, but there's not much wrong with you. But here you are, in a private room, with servants to bring you all you need, and friends to smother the place with flowers and gifts. I've seen women with killing diseases, living in overcrowded tenements, with not even a bed to themselves, and nowhere to go for so much as the sight of a daisy but the public parks, if they can drag themselves there."

The deep sincerity in his voice moved

me, but I was angry and wanted to hit back, too.

"I'm very sorry for such women," I said quietly. "But I should think you could do them more good than I could. This quiet, pleasant country practice must be quite a change for you after the Glasgow slums."

I could see by his expression that my shaft had hit him really hard and I was instantly remorseful.

He looked away from me and set his lips. Then he said, in a controlled way: "I had my reasons for coming here."

"I'm sure you had," I said quickly, and added: "So won't you believe that *I* have *my* reasons for staying at home?"

He met my eyes with his stabbing glance. "Yes, I believe it," he said. "But I'm thinking they're no very sound reasons."

"Oh, you're incorrigible!" I cried, then burst out laughing.

He looked surprised, then continued to eye me soberly. "You heard me agreeing that you were beautiful," he said, very quietly. "And that's another unfair advantage you have, Miss D'alquen of Westings."

"Call me Silla," I said, smiling at him. "And I'll call you Alan. It's silly to be so formal when we've been so frank with each other."

At that point Sister came back into the room.

"You've got quite a good colour, Miss D'alquen," she remarked in congratulatory tones.

"Yes, there's nothing much wrong with this patient now, Sister," declared Alan. He gave me a nod and marched off.

After that I was allowed more visitors. My father and Dr. Robbie came to see me again, and Mrs. Appleby, the vicar's wife, and one or two others. Sister shook her head and frowned, but when the thin, plain assistant Nurse Jones told me that a young couple named Price were asking to see me I asked her to let them come up at once.

These must be Nanny's newly discovered grandchildren. Well, I had things to say to the young man he might not care to hear. I watched the door in anticipation. I'm not quite sure what I expected to see. I think some arrogant lout accompanied by a plump but youthfully pretty edition of Nanny herself.

They were so different. He was a slim, dark young man, appearing unaware of his amazing good looks, his manner almost diffident, in fact. She was small and slight, with the kind of hair Americans call 'strawberry blonde'. It may have been their casual dress of jeans and sport shirts that made them seem so young. But his cap of black curls and curling black eyelashes — far too good for a man — and the way her hair was tied in a top-knot with pale blue ribbon, certainly helped in the effect.

He was holding an armful of glorious golden roses, and managing to look quite at his ease with them, and she carried a big box of chocolates decorated with a huge red bow. They brought a kind of fairy-tale glamour into the austere little room.

"Hullo," said the boy, with a charming smile. "It's awfully good of you to see us. You must hate me like the Black Death or something, after what I did to you yesterday. Letta has been telling me I ought to be in a home, but honestly I thought we were in the unpeopled countryside. I never expected to find one car in the lane, let alone two."

"He was quite, quite mad," said the girl, in a small voice that was yet silvery clear. "He might have killed us all."

"I should have gone to eternity in delightful company," said Adrian. "Except for the rugged type with the Scottish accent, of course. But what a mercy it was he turned out to be a doctor. For a ghastly moment or two we thought you were dead."

"I nearly flung my arms round the man and kissed him, when he said you weren't," said the girl, sitting gracefully in the only chair.

"So did I," said her brother. "God! That would have given him a shock." He grinned and seated himself on the side of the bed. His diffident manner seemed to have vanished.

"Flowers for a lovely lady," he said, handing me the roses. Then his voice changed comically. "I'm ever so sorry, really I am. I didn't go for to do it, miss."

Letta's laugh was a pleasure to hear. "Isn't he a fool!" she said, handing me the chocolates. "Darling, I hope you aren't on a diet. Though I'm sure you have no earthly reason to be. Your figure looked divine to me."

"How lucky I am to have somebody to say these things for me," said Adrian, giving me a glance that was amorous and yet inoffensive.

All this time I had had no chance to do more than utter some conventional murmurs. Now I said: "I accept your apologies with these wonderful roses

71

and the chocolates, which I shall certainly pig into. Now do tell me, please, how you came to visit your grandmother after all these years of silence."

"What a woman!" exclaimed Adrian. "Really quite a marathon going round the dear old soul!"

I opened my eyes rather wide, to hear Nanny Price so described.

Letta gave her sweet laugh again. "Darling, won't it be awful if I ever grow like that. After all, I must have some of the same genes, or whatever they are."

"Oh, you're not the same type at all," said her brother. "You take after our mother's people. Father always said *I* resembled *his* family."

"I can't see that either of you are in the least like Nanny," I said. I looked at Adrian. "But you do remind me of somebody. Perhaps it's a photograph of your father or grandfather I've seen at some time or other."

I saw them exchange a quick glance

and remembered suddenly the fate of William Price. I wondered if they knew about that.

"But I must have my roses put in water at once," I said quickly. And I expect you'd like some tea."

Nurse Jones brought a vase for the flowers, then tea, with reasonably thin bread and butter and some delicious cakes sent by Mrs. Budge. In no time those two made a gay little party of the occasion. Hearing the laughter, Sister looked in with a gaze of disapproving enquiry, but her severe expression soon relaxed before the charm they turned on her and she withdrew smiling.

They told me in a light-hearted way that they had known nothing of their father's origins till quite recently. All that he had told them was that he had lived in the country as a boy and had run away from a possessive and domineering mother when he was in his teens. Then they had met an old friend of his, who had helped him set up as a printer in a small way when he had first married their mother, and he had told them about Westings having been the place their father had run from and where his mother had been some sort of privileged servant.

"We were both between plays, so we thought it might be fun to look the place up. They told us at the pub that Nanny Price was still at the 'big house', and we felt we simply had to call and say 'Hullo Granny' to her," said Adrian.

"She must have been very surprised," I remarked.

"The queer thing is, she wasn't," said Adrian. "At least, not as surprised as I thought she would be." He turned to his sister. "What was it she said, Letta?"

"Better late than never. Perhaps the dead'll rest quiet now," said Letta, with a passable imitation of Nanny's voice. "Rather creepy, wasn't it?"

It certainly cast rather a chill over me.

"Anyhow, now we've found our long lost ancestress we mean to be very dutiful," continued Adrian. "Your father has been awfully kind, particularly under the circumstances — which I shall not mention again." He covered his face with his outspread fingers.

"Fancy! There's actually some talk of us renting the lodge at Westings," put in Letta. "It will be simply marvellous to have a home again, even if we have to furnish that sweet little house with old boxes or something."

"We think Westings is fabulous," declared Adrian. "It will be heaven to live in the willow cabin at your gate, so to speak."

My heart warmed to them. I decided that it would be fun to have them at the lodge, and said so.

"Well, if *you're* in favour the matter must be as good as settled," cried Adrian. "Talk about turning the other cheek." He put on the cockney voice again. "You're a bloomin' h'angel lidy!" Then he was suddenly serious. "Honestly, I don't know how to thank you," he said simply.

"Then don't try," I said.

"Come along, Letta, we'd better go, before that Sister comes and slays us with a scalpel," said Adrian. He seized my hand and kissed it quickly.

Slightly embarrassed, I said: "Letta is an unusual name."

"It's really Violet, darling," she said, pulling a face. "But how could I go on the stage with a name like Violet Price?"

They turned at the doorway and waved gaily, and with their going a blankness and silence descended as if a curtain had come down.

4

NEXT day I went home. My father came in the Humber to fetch me, driven by Friedrich, and Matron herself stood smiling and waving from the step as we drove off. Remembering Alan's words, I felt faintly guilty about that, but, after all, D'alquen money and effort had been largely responsible for the little hospital's existence. My grandfather had laid the foundation stone. There was a plaque in the entrance hall to commemorate the event.

Nanny was at the door to receive us at Westings, looking monumental in her vast black dress. Her short fat hands, clasped on her mountainous stomach, were marked with the brown blotches of old age.

"Welcome home, Miss Silla," she said, in that voice of hers that always seemed too small for her personality. "You're looking peaked. Some of my beetroot tonic will soon set you up again."

"Now Nanny! Remember what Dr. Laird said. No more dosing," said my father good-naturedly.

"A lot he knows about it, Sir James," said Nanny, her half-buried black eyes gleaming angrily. "A boy like that! Why, I was giving people my doses — *and* with very good results — years before he was born."

I had been watching her keenly, for any signs of abnormality, but she seemed exactly the same as usual to me.

"I met your grandchildren yesterday, Nanny," I said, wanting to change the subject. "They seem charming. You must have been thrilled to see them."

"As to that, I can't be expected to love them I never set eyes on before," said Nanny. "But it was meant their line should be brought back to Westings."

"Your poor William has been dead for fifty years, Nanny," said my father gently. "It can't really matter to him whether or not his grandchildren come to Westings."

Nanny's face took on the expressionlessness of a fat yellow doll. But there was a note of cold contempt in her thin voice as she said: "William was a fool, Sir James." Then she turned and waddled away.

I was puzzled. That last remark of hers didn't match at all with the ghost-seeing described by Friedrich. Could it be that the old woman had forgotten that episode? And if so, was this an alarming symptom?

My father showed no sign of surprise or alarm, however. He turned his attention to my well-being and begged me not to exert myself too soon, for I had already noticed various things requiring attention, as I looked round the hall. The arrangement of the flowers, some dust on the polished treads of the stairs.

Then the dogs erupted into the room and as I stooped to meet them, I was aware of the throbbing in my head and knew that I was not quite fit yet. But it was good to be home.

Later, my father brought up the subject of the letting of the lodge to Adrian and Letta.

"Personally, I feel like sending that young man about his business, for all his charm," he said, as we sat at lunch. "But there's Nanny to be considered. It's right that she should have her own family about her in her old age. There's the girl, too. She can't be blamed for her brother's conduct."

"I thought Nanny didn't seem very enthusiastic about them," I remarked.

"Nanny Price doesn't belong to this modern world, Silla," said my father. "She's one of the old kind of family servant with a fund of feudal loyalty to the family that employs her. But blood counts, and these young people are her only real relations."

"So you're going to let them have

the lodge," I said, realising where his remarks were leading.

"Yes. If you've no objection. They seem keen on doing it up themselves. I only hope they don't ruin the little house. But perhaps you can tactfully guide their tastes as much as possible."

But there was no need for that. Adrian and Letta's ideas ran to white paint and simplicity. They came down next day with tins of paint and brushes and a picnic-basket, saying they were too impatient to wait for a legal agreement to be drawn up.

"Of course, Sir James's word is good enough for us," said Adrian, perching gracefully on a window-ledge, where old Mrs. Benson had always placed her geraniums, the choice plants — I had always suspected — from our own greenhouses.

"Letta wants window-boxes," he told me, swinging a well-shaped foot in a disreputable sandal.

"And a hanging basket in that adorable little porch," said Letta,

81

who looked devastatingly pretty in frayed jeans and a faded old shirt, with her bright hair showing beneath a black nylon scarf tied gipsy fashion round her head. "Is that allowed?" she asked, turning to me appealingly.

"It will look charming," I said.

"Oh, it's all such fun!" cried Letta, flinging up her arms then hugging herself. "Adrian, let's have a house-warming when we really move in."

Adrian wrinkled his nose fastidiously. "Oh God! Not the gang!" he said. "I was hoping to get away from them."

"Yes, so was I," said his sister quickly. "I was thinking of inviting Granny and Sir James, if it wouldn't bore him too much. And, Silla, you'll come, won't you darling?"

She spoke with an engaging diffidence, and I scarcely noticed her familiar way of addressing me. After all, she could scarcely have called me 'Miss Silla', as her grandmother did, and 'Miss D'alquen' would have seemed stiff and formal coming from her. I remembered that actors and actresses were said to use first names all the time and call practically anyone 'darling'.

I said I should love to come to their house-warming and I was sure my father would, too.

In a couple of days they had actually moved in, for I had helped them furnish the place with a few pieces of furniture tucked away in the attics of Westings. But before they could hold their party several events occurred.

First, I gave a little party myself. On the day I came home from the cottage hospital my father had said: "As soon as you feel up to entertaining, Silla, we must have young Laird to dine."

Secretly pleased, I laughed and answered: "He might not come, Daddy. I don't think he approves of our kind. Considers us parasites or something."

"Oh, he's a Socialist, is he," said my father equably. "Well, I don't see why his politics should stand in the way of his accepting a civil invitation."

"I'll ask him, of course, if you wish

it," I said. "How about having the Applebys at the same time? And Miss Peach. That will make it even. Shouldn't we ask Dr. Robbie too, though?"

"No. I like Robbie to come on his own," answered my father. "And we ought not to take both doctors off duty."

Rather to my surprise, Alan accepted my invitation, writing me the briefest of notes in a clear firm hand-writing. "Thank you for your invitation. I should like to come. Sincerely yours, Alan Laird." I smiled as I read it.

I had no doubt the vicar and his wife would accept. They scarcely went anywhere, except on parochial affairs, and dinner at Westings was quite an occasion to them. And I was pretty sure of Miss Peach.

Mary Peach was a retired schoolmistress living in the village on a pension, and was the daughter of an admiral who had distinguished himself somehow in the First World War and subsequently been killed. She was a large boned but good-looking woman of sixty, who went in for mannish clothes and short haircuts that didn't really hide an underlying femininity. She had a beautiful little garden and kept her small house exquisitely neat and pretty in spite of her two dogs and three cats. She was intelligent and sensitive and I liked her more and more the better I came to know her.

I dressed with especial care for my guests that evening. Or rather for one of my guests. My white and green cocktail dress was plain enough, but I piled my hair on top of my head and put some emerald earrings that had been my mother's in my ears, and touched the lobes and my wrists and throat with an expensive perfume that I kept for special occasions.

"Why you look quite queenly," whispered Mrs. Appleby, when Friedrich conducted her into the hall a step or two in front of her husband. They were the first arrivals.

I wondered if that was the effect I really wanted to achieve, but I smiled my gratitude for the compliment.

Then Alan came, and he gave me exactly the same kind of look as on the first morning of our acquaintance. A startled stare, then a stern lowering of the eyes. But somehow it satisfied me.

We had dinner in the garden room, a smallish room with a pleasant view of the garden from its one long window.

While Miss Peach told an amusing anecdote about one of her cats, I looked at Alan as unobtrusively as I could.

Relaxed, as now, his face was more youthful, but it was a strong face rather than a handsome one. I wondered why it appealed to me so much.

"I make no apology for my menagerie," concluded Mary, in her rather deep voice, that always seemed to have a note of wry amusement in it. "After all, Adam lived with animals before God gave him Eve. I know the sexes are reversed in my case, but as the

Almighty isn't likely to present me with an Adam at this late day, I do very well with my four-footed company."

"But Miss Peach," said Mrs. Appleby, who took everything literally, "when Adam had to make do with the company of animals there were no other human beings."

Miss Peach gave a laugh. "Well, there are no human beings as far as I'm concerned," she said. "None who would want to live with me, I mean."

"I feel sure you are mistaken there," said my father with a smile.

I saw a faint flush darken Mary's sunburn, and for a moment she looked shy and almost young. Then she was laughing again.

"Well, perhaps the boot is on the other foot a little, if one can make such a muddy metaphor," she said. "It's true that there aren't many people *I'd* care to live with."

"But there are some," said Mrs. Appleby earnestly.

"One or two," admitted Miss Peach,

and she glanced at my father and away again.

It struck me, not for the first time, that she admired him a good deal and was very appreciative of the old-fashioned courtesies he showed her. It even crossed my mind that my father might consider marrying her, as an insurance against loneliness, when I myself was married. The thought gave me a stab of pain. To think of Miss Peach as mistress of Westings during the rest of my father's lifetime filled me with alarm and dismay. I was not being selfish, I told myself. Nice as she was, she wasn't really suitable. Besides, there was no need for my father to be lonely. I intended to make Westings still my principal home after I was married. Julian, as its heir, could hardly object.

I looked the length of the polished refectory table at my father, sitting at the other end. He was looking serene and handsome in the black velvet jacket he loved to wear in the evenings. He met my eyes and smiled. Of course he wouldn't marry Mary Peach, I thought, relieved. I had been absurd.

The vicar had said something about the necessity for adaptability in living with others. He was a quiet colourless man, very fond of his wife, who was pretty in a faded workaday way.

"They tell me that adaptability is the secret of successful marriage, and that women are better at it than men," said Alan, in a cautious voice.

"They have to be, poor dears!" remarked Mary.

"Whither thou goest I will go, and where thou lodgest I will lodge. Thy people shall be my people and thy God my God!" quoted Mrs. Appleby.

"Yes, dear, but do remember that Ruth said that to her mother-in-law, not her husband," said the vicar with a slight smile.

"Of course. I know that, Leonard," said his wife. "But the principle is the same."

"I don't think I could say that

honestly to anyone," I remarked lightly.

"Oh yes, dear I'm sure you will, when the time comes," said Mrs. Appleby.

"Really?" I said politely, and met the brilliant gaze of Alan.

He held my eyes with his for what seemed a long time but was probably only a second, then looked down at the debris of dessert on his plate.

I rose, rather taking the company by surprise. "Coffee on the terrace, I thought, as it's such a lovely evening. Mrs. Appleby, you may need your stole," I said.

She was in a flowery short-sleeved dress, while Mary wore a severely tailored blouse with her black skirt.

It was still only very early July and the evenings were long. My father had some old-fashioned habits and tastes but sitting over the port was not one of them. The vicar was a one glass man and I couldn't imagine Alan being much addicted to wine. Soon we were all sitting outside in the softly scented air, while Friedrich handed round coffee.

In front there were rosebuds. Beyond, the grass sloped smoothly down to the lake, and across the water I could see the eighteenth-century gazebo crowning the little hill that marked the limit of Westings Park. By turning my head I could see the great cedar beside the house looking dark and full of shadows. I sat there beside Alan with a curious sense of peace and well-being. I had no desire to talk.

But it wasn't long before the older folk wanted to go in and play bridge.

"What shall we do?" I asked Alan. "Stay here till it's dark? Look at television? There's a record-player, if you care for music. Do you dance, by the way?"

"Very badly," he said. "I'll not inflict my great feet on you. It's very pleasant out here. We could maybe walk round the grounds."

"Yes," I said. "We could do that. But we'd better keep to the neater paths. I'm not wearing the right shoes for rough ground."

"They're very pretty, though," he said, looking down my flimsy sandals. "And very small."

"I didn't know you could pay compliments," I said, smiling at him.

"It's the simple truth," he answered shortly.

We walked slowly, side by side, pausing to sniff at the roses, then I led him along a path that went by a devious way down to the lake.

"That part-time cook you mentioned knows her job," he said abruptly.

"I'm glad you enjoyed your dinner," I said demurely. "But as a matter of fact I cooked most of it."

"You can cook!" he exclaimed in surprise. He sounded pleased, too.

"I can," I said. "And I do, when I have to. But I hope those occasions are going to get fewer and fewer."

"You won't find servants easier to come by in the future," he told me, frowning. "But no doubt you won't need so many when you leave Westings."

"When I leave Westings?" I repeated, startled. I turned to look at him, as I had taken a step ahead, with the narrowness of the path.

"When you marry, I mean," he said, startling me again. He added: "You're bound to marry, you know, whatever you think now."

I glanced at him quickly. "You haven't considered that I might marry a rich man," I said.

He shook his head. "You'll not do that," he declared. "You'd never marry for money."

"Oh? No, I wouldn't marry just for money," I agreed.

It was true. I was not marrying Julian for the sake of his quite large income and his holdings in Judsons, but for the sake of Westings and to make my father happy, and because I was fond of him and he could insure that I continued to lead the kind of life I enjoyed.

It was strange that none of these

reasons seemed good enough suddenly.

The path had widened a little and Alan was beside me again. I looked up at him and my sandals tripped me on a rise in the level of the ground. I staggered and clutched his arm and laughed a little breathlessly. He put an arm round me quickly to steady me.

I stopped laughing and my heart began to thud. We stared at each other and a thrush burst out singing from a nearby tree. Then I was in his arms and his lips were pressing hard on mine. My own arms seemed to lift themselves and go round his neck.

"Well!" I gasped, when he released me. Then I smiled at him shakily.

His face seemed to be glowing with an inward warmth and light. He seized my hand and held it in both his own.

"Drusilla," he said quickly. "There are things you ought to know about me before I can ask you to marry me."

Sanity returned to me with a leap.

"But Alan," I cried. "I can't *marry* you."

I never saw a man change so quickly. For a moment he looked stunned, then his face became stiff and cold and proud.

"I see," he said harshly. "I'm good enough to amuse yourself with, but not for anything more permanent. Well, Miss D'alquen of Westings, I'm no gigolo."

The very idea of anybody thinking he was seemed so absurd that I gave a short explosive laugh.

He flushed darkly, turned and strode away.

"Alan!" I exclaimed. "I didn't mean — " Before I could finish he had stopped and my heart lifted.

"Please make my apologies to Sir James," he rapped out over his shoulder, and marched off round the path and out of my sight.

This time I let him go. I was shaken. As much by my own emotions as by his behaviour. I walked on for a little way by myself, telling Alan in my mind what I had really meant. Then I felt angry with him for taking offence, without giving me the chance to explain. But could I really explain anything? I asked myself this while remembering that I had practically flung myself into one man's arms when I was engaged to another.

It was dusk and I was shivering a little in spite of my stole when I went in at last.

In the hall, my father, the vicar and Mary Peach were seated at the card-table. Mrs. Appleby, who was evidently dummy, sat in one of the armchairs knitting what appeared to be a tea-cosy in thick yellow wool.

"All alone?" she said, looking up with a smile as I entered.

"Dr. Laird had to leave," I said, trying to sound as natural as possible. "He asked me to make his apologies to you, Daddy."

My father looked up from his cards and murmured: "Pity!" Then his glance sharpened. "Have you been overdoing it, darling?" he asked. "You look rather strained. Why not go to bed now? I'm sure our guests will forgive you."

"Of course," said Mary.

"It's the result of that shocking accident," remarked Mrs. Appleby. "I've been telling Sir James, it was more than Christian of him to let the lodge to those two young people, even if they are old Mrs. Price's grandchildren."

"Can one be more than Christian?" the vicar asked gently.

"Actors too!" exclaimed his wife, unheeding.

Mary laughed. "The village would have preferred them to be television personalities," she said.

"They have had some small parts in television plays," I told her. "I think that's why I keep having the feeling I've met Adrian Price before."

Then the door opened and Friedrich came in. I saw at once that something was wrong, for his face was more than usually pale and a nerve was twitching in one cheek.

"Please, is Dr. Laird still here, Miss

Silla?" he asked anxiously.

"No," I answered. "He had to leave."

"What is it, Friedrich?" asked my father sharply.

"It is Mrs. Price, sir," said Friedrich in a low voice, bending over him.

"She's ill?" said my father, rising.

"This afternoon, her stomach — it was upset," said Friedrich. "She moaned and she groaned, but she would not have the doctor come."

"And now she's worse?" said my father quickly.

"Now I think, sir, she is dead," said Friedrich simply.

5

FRIEDRICH'S fears were justified. Nanny Price was dead, though at first I couldn't believe it.

"Ring for Dr. Robertson immediately, Friedrich," ordered my father. Then asked quickly: "Where is Mrs. Price?"

"In the housekeeper's room, Sir James, sitting in her chair," answered the Austrian.

"Excuse me," said my father to our guests. "I must go to her at once."

"Perhaps a woman will be needed," said Mrs. Appleby, laying down her knitting and jumping up.

I remembered my duties. "Of course," I said. "I'll come with you, Daddy."

Mary Peach stopped me with an arm round my shoulders. "You're not well enough, my dear," she said.

"No," said my father, giving her a

grateful glance. "If you'll be so kind, Mrs. Appleby."

"Maude is very experienced," the vicar assured me. "It's better she should go. Dear me! A sad business! But of course at Mrs. Price's age — "

They were all very kind, but I had the feeling Alan would not have approved of my being so sheltered from one of the harsh realities of life.

Dr. Robbie arrived and spent quite a long time in the housekeeper's room, and then was closeted with my father in his study. Mrs. Appleby had soon rejoined us, shaking her head gravely, and she and the vicar and Miss Peach waited with me, though they seemed uncertain whether the more tactful thing was to go or stay. I was glad of their company, however.

At last Dr. Robbie went and my father came into the hall. He looked white and drawn and I realised suddenly how important this old woman had once been to him and for how long a time she had been a part of his background. I went to him and took his hand and pressed it and he smiled at me faintly.

"Poor Nanny has gone," he said quietly. "But Dr. Robertson thinks she didn't suffer. It was heart failure and quite sudden. Thank you for your help, Mrs. Appleby. Vicar, I'll arrange with you about the funeral later. I've tried to get in touch with the young Prices, but apparently they're in London visiting their agent, and won't be back till tomorrow. In any case, they scarcely know their grandmother. This is a D'alquen responsibility. Mrs. Price has served our family devotedly for sixty years."

There was emotion in his voice, but he controlled it.

"It was good of you to stay, Mary," he murmured, turning to Miss Peach. And again I saw that look of shy pleasure on her face.

When the guests had gone he patted my shoulder and said tenderly: "to bed, darling. You're looking like your own ghost."

"How about you, Daddy? You don't look too robust yourself," I said.

"I'm all right," he told me. "I'll wait up for a little while." He hesitated, then added: "An ambulance will be here shortly to take poor Nanny away."

I was startled but, at the same time, relieved. "Is that necessary?" I asked.

"Apparently so, under the circumstances," he answered. "You see, this was an unexpected death."

"Do you mean there will have to be an autopsy?" I said.

"I suppose so," said my father reluctantly. "But don't worry about it, Silla. You be off to bed. And sleep soundly. No need to weep for Nanny. She has had a long and at least a comfortable life."

But when I had gone to my room I flung myself on the bed, still in my cocktail dress, and wept bitterly. Not, I'm afraid, for the death of our old servant and friend, but because Alan

Laird had been ready to love me and now, thanks to my stupid laughter, would probably hate me for ever.

In the morning things seemed brighter, as they always do. I even asked myself why on earth I had upset myself over an arrogant, humourless young man, who had had no right to assume I was his just for the asking. But I didn't want him to think of me as the kind of girl who plays with a man's emotions for fun, so as soon as I was dressed I wrote him a little note and asked Friedrich to see that it was put through the letter-box at Woodside that morning.

"Dear Alan," I had written, "Please believe that I had no intention of hurting you yesterday evening, but I'm afraid you might have misunderstood a laugh that was, I admit, mis-timed. It was not really directed at you. Drusilla."

After that, my spirits rose a little. But they were doomed to fall again.

My father, who was seated at breakfast in the little morning-room, greeted me affectionately, but did not have much to say during the meal. He read his mail and occasionally picked up *The Times* glanced at it and put it down again. He was looking heavy-eyed, as if he hadn't slept well.

When I rose from the table after my usual fruit-juice, toast and coffee, he said quickly: "Don't go, Silla. There's something I have to tell you."

"Is it about Nanny?" I asked with sudden uneasy premonition.

He nodded. "Yes. There has to be an autopsy. You see, Dr. Robbie thinks her death was not entirely natural."

It was then that my sense of foreboding grew. I shivered as if the cold black shadow of the great cedar had fallen on me. "Murder?" I cried.

He stared at me as if he had caught some of the horror I was feeling.

"God, no, child!" he said. "Don't look like that. Nobody suspects even suicide. It was undoubtedly what will be called misadventure, if it comes to an inquest. In a way, I blame young Laird."

"What?" I exclaimed, feeling a new shock.

"He was so tactless with her over her precious brews. I think she wanted to prove him wrong. You see, Robbie is pretty sure her heart failure was caused by digitalis. There was some left in a glass in her room. At least, that's what he thinks it is. I've no doubt poor Nanny took too large a dose by mistake, or if it was a normal one, that her old heart couldn't stand it."

This explanation seemed very likely. My reason told me so, but the dark foreboding continued to depress me, even when I thought that it was fortunate for my father he hadn't been the victim.

When Adrian and Letta returned and were told of their grandmother's death they expressed surprise and regret but made no pretence of any real grief.

Letta looked at my father with big child-like eyes, as we sat together in the hall. "Poor, poor Granny!" she said. "I'm terribly sorry. But I hope nobody expects me to go and look at her, because I couldn't." She shuddered delicately.

"Of course nobody expects it, my dear," said my father. "Anyone so young and charming should have nothing to do with death."

I remembered at a future time how he had said that.

"Oh thank you," cried Letta, smiling. "You say nice things so beautifully."

"You were always very good to Granny," said Adrian. "And we do thank you for it."

"It's we who have to thank her," said my father. "She spent the greater part of a long life working for us here at Westings. We shall miss her very much. And that reminds me — "

He hesitated and appeared slightly embarrassed, which was a very rare thing.

I understand from her solicitor — who is mine too — that your grandmother has left me her savings," he continued. "It amounts to nearly a thousand pounds. Of course she made the will before she knew she had descendants living, and you must allow me to make the money over to you two."

For a moment Adrian looked at my father blankly, as if taken by surprise. Then he shook his handsome head.

"Nothing doing, sir," he said firmly. "I don't think Granny would have made any different arrangement if she had lived longer. We were strangers to her really. You and your family, and Westings Court meant everything to her. Besides, I know you have let us have the lodge on very generous terms, for her sake, and I shouldn't blame you if now you're rather regretting it." He grinned rather ruefully.

"Not at all," said my father courteously. "You mustn't think that. It will be a pleasant change for my daughter to have young people about. But I hope you will change your mind about accepting your grandmother's money. What does your sister say about that?"

"Adrian's quite right. We couldn't accept it," said Letta, shaking her bright head.

I caught a flicker of regret in her eyes, however, and it made me think that the couple were probably often hard up. Financial security was never one of the charms of the acting profession. I decided to suggest to my father, when we were alone, that he should use his persuasions on Letta alone, to get the young people to accept Nanny's little hoard.

"I'm afraid it will be no use, Sir James," said Adrian.

He was looking elegant in a well-cut suit today, having just come from London, a sophisticated young man of the world. But now he put on that air of boyish diffidence that had impressed me in hospital. "But there are what I believe are known as 'the effects'," he said with a shy smile. "Granny said something about boxes of letters and old papers and photographs she wanted me to look through after she had gone. It's strange, but she mentioned them only a few days ago. She seemed to think they would be of family interest to Letta and me."

Again I thought my father seemed slightly embarrassed. But he said quickly: "Of course you are welcome to anything of your grandmother's you care to have. Nothing has been touched. But I have heard officially now that there is to be an inquest. I expect you have been notified also. I don't think anything may be removed till it's over."

Letta leaned forward. She had gone a little pale. "Then — then they'll find out how she died?" she said.

"Apparently the post-mortem revealed that she had taken a fatal dose of digitalis," he said. "I suppose the inquest is to decide how she managed to do that. Dr. Robbie has a theory I feel may be correct."

Adrian looked at him sharply. "What's that?" he asked.

"Nanny had become very absent-minded as well as obstinate," said my father. "The glass the police found contained dregs of a very powerful mixture of digitalis. Dr. Robbie thinks she had forgotten the correct amount of dilution necessary, but took the stuff just to prove herself in the right."

"I see," said Adrian thoughtfully. "Yes, I should think that probably is what happened. Of course we didn't know her well, but she did strike us as being a bit odd at times, didn't she Letta? Things she said about our grandfather for instance."

"Oh yes. They just didn't fit with his having been just a groom," said Letta. "Delusions of grandeur I called it, poor darling."

My father cleared his throat. "Well, old age often brings these things, unfortunately," he said dismissingly.

I had a reply to my little note to Alan that day. He wrote simply: "Your note was kindly meant, no doubt, but I know very well when I have made a fool of myself. You can be sure I shall not commit the same folly again, under any provocation," and signed himself: "Yours sincerely, Alan Laird."

I didn't know whether to laugh or cry, as I read it, in the privacy of my own room. This was undoubtedly what my friends at school would have called 'the brush-off'. And a good thing too, I told myself. There was really no room for Alan Laird in the plans I had for my own future.

As a postscript to his brief letter he had added, with characteristic forthrightness: "I cannot say I am exactly sorry for the death of your old housekeeper. It was better she should poison herself than somebody else."

In imagination, I could hear his rather deep voice with the Scottish accent saying that plain piece of common sense, and it gave me an extraordinary sharp pang.

I didn't attend the inquest on Lucy

Millicent Price, as she was officially called during the proceedings. I had a bad headache, an aftermath, perhaps of the concussion. The coroner's view turned out to be substantially the same as my father's however, and poor Nanny was declared to have died by misadventure.

I was well enough to go to the funeral. My father was glad of my company, I think, and felt it was my duty to go, in any case. He and I and the other faithful servant of Westings, Friedrich, supported the two young Prices as mourners. The local press had been represented at the inquest and there were paragraphs about it in the local papers, but the affair had attracted little notice, and the only people in the church were Mrs. Dean, our cook, with one or two other of the local women, and a few old men who remembered Nanny as a young woman.

It was an overcast day, and as Mr. Appleby, tall and impressive in his white surplice, stood, under the shadow of an ancient yew at the gate to receive the coffin, and the Norman tower of the little grey church sent out its solemn bell note, I saw Letta shiver and clutch at her brother's arm.

She was wearing a small black hat on her marigold coloured hair. Her black dress was of a schoolgirl simplicity. She looked like a beautiful orphan child who had been flung on the world and was begging it with scared beseeching eyes not to be unkind.

Afterwards, over biscuits and sherry at the house, she became quite gay, tossing aside the little hat, then clapping it on at an entirely different angle and doing an impersonation of a Victorian governess who had accidentally got tipsy. Then she was stricken with self-reproach, as she reminded herself of the occasion.

"That's an attractive girl," said my father, when they had gone. "She reminds me of Angelique."

Angelique was an exquisite marmalade

kitten I had recently acquired, whose moods of wild playfulness alternated with wistful appeal. Rollo, the old retriever, adored her, and even the rather surly Davis was obviously quite fascinated. The whole household spoiled her, but Mary Peach declared that her character wouldn't suffer as a consequence. Quite the opposite, in fact.

"Cats are unspoilable, anyway," she said with one of her laughs. "They know their own worth from the start and aren't affected by your opinion of it. They need love, though, and they'll love you back, if they think you deserve it. Then they'll try to please you, but only to a reasonable extent and they'll expect you to reciprocate."

"What sensible creatures they must be!" my father had remarked, listening to her. "It's a pity we human beings aren't the same. There's a lot of love wasted on undeserving men and women and a great deal of unreason shown in the process."

"Yes," said Mary, with a faint blush. "If love can ever be really wasted. I grant you the unreason, though."

It was on the day of the funeral that I took Adrian and Letta up to Nanny's room. It was one of the darkest rooms in the house and full of heavy old furniture. Several times I had suggested she should change but she had always refused, saying she was used to the room and that anywhere else would seem strange to her.

"Crikey!" said Adrian, gazing round him. "I've never been in her bedroom before. "All that ponderous mahogany! It looks like a set for a Victorian melo-drama." He turned to Letta, who was wrinkling her small nose distastefully in the doorway. "Come inside, darling. Whatever it is, it's not Bluebeard's chamber," he said.

The atmosphere was stuffy and permeated with a smell of camphor mixed with lavender water and worn clothes, so I went to the window and opened it wide. The time of day seemed later than it actually was, because of the heavy cloud and the stillness of the air. The nearness of the great cedar helped in this effect, too. I glanced sideways at the old tree and my scalp pricked, my heart gave a terrified leap. For a brief instant I had thought I saw a long black bundle hanging from the lowest branch and swinging gently. I gave a cry and drew back sharply, then turned to find Adrian beside me. I must have looked white and shocked, for his own face suddenly reflected this.

"The cedar! I thought I saw — " I gasped. Then I checked myself. But Adrian finished the sentence for me.

"Something nasty! Not Grandfather William? Oh, what a thrill!" He spoke with a lightness that was belied by his expression.

He seemed to brace himself then turned his head with a curiously jerky movement towards the cedar. I gathered up my courage and looked, too. There was no dangling shape, nothing but the old dark branches standing rather stiffly in the sultry evening.

I heard Adrian let out a breath and could sense how he relaxed.

"Pity!" he said. "I can't see anything unusual. I should have adored seeing the Westings' ghost."

"It must have been nerves," I said quickly, still feeling shaken. "Or imagination, and knowing that Nanny had seen — " I stopped again, and turned back to the room, to find Letta standing rigid with terror.

"Adrian," she cried in a high voice. "I can't stand it. I can't. I can't."

He strode past me and seized her by the shoulders and shook her, none too gently.

"Stop it," he said sharply. "It's all nonsense. There are no such things as ghosts."

"There are, there are," she wailed. "There were those footsteps at that old theatre, and — "

"All right, all right," he said, more sympathetically. "But if there are such things they can't hurt you. They're

117

nothing. Mere shadows, impressions. They don't *matter*, darling."

"I'm awfully sorry to have scared you, Letta," I said, as soothingly as I could, considering the state of my own nerves. "I expect it was just fancy. I've had some shocks lately, and maybe the concussion I had is still affecting me."

I didn't believe this explanation, and I don't now, but Adrian pounced on it.

"There. It's all my fault, indirectly," he said. "Now, my pet, you go downstairs with Silla, and I'll look through Granny's things by myself."

Letta accepted this suggestion with relief and, once away from the sombre room, quickly recovered her spirits. Nanny Price's few possessions were sorted out and disposed of, but Adrian still refused to take my father's legacy from him, and his sister, when tactfully pressed, said no she couldn't, for Adrian had made up his mind they mustn't. It confirmed me in an impression I had received, that Letta was very much under her brother's influence and, in fact, rather dominated by him.

I didn't see a great deal of the young couple, because I was careful not to intrude on them at the lodge. Life seemed to have got back to normal at Westings. Nanny's duties had become very slight with her increasing age and stoutness, and I didn't much miss her contribution to the work of the house. My father soon put aside the sadness he had felt and became quite his old self. I played tennis in my free time, and rode a little and visited a little, and went up to London for shopping and a matinee. All this time I saw nothing of Alan. But once, when I went to tea at the Vicarage, I had news of him.

"Rather a rude young man!" remarked Mrs. Appleby, handing me a cup covered with roses. "But dear Dr. Robertson seems to think highly of him. Perhaps marriage will improve him."

6

MY hand jerked so that the tea spilled over. After Mrs. Appleby had fussed a little over giving me a clean saucer I brought her back to the remark that had startled me.

"What made you mention marriage in connection with Alan Laird?" I asked, keeping such a fixed smile on my face that it quite ached.

"Well, dear," said my hostess, cutting a rather heavy-looking cake with a bit of a flourish, "he's been seeing quite a lot of one of the nurses from the Cottage Hospital, it seems, and of course people are drawing their own onclusions."

"Really?" I said, displaying bright interest. "I wonder which nurse it is."

"I think her name is Paul," replied

Mrs. Appleby. "Sylvia Paul. Or is it Susan? Do you know her?"

"Oh yes. I'm sure I remember her," I said.

Nurse Paul was the pretty dark girl I had thought looked like a sophisticated kitten.

"I always think it's a good thing when a doctor marries a nurse," remarked the vicar's wife, passing me the cake. "They're bound to have so much in common. She'll be able to help him in his work, if they do make a match of it."

I made sounds of assent, but I thought to myself that I knew Nurse Paul's type. She was all out to add scalps to her girdle in the sex war. She would probably lead her husband a fine dance. Alan would have his work cut out to manage *her*. "And serve him right," I told myself viciously. Then I thought it would be terrible for him, and couldn't bear it, and Mrs. Appleby's cake seemed to be choking me.

Next day, when I was exercising Jessup, my pony, I guided him in the direction of Woodside. My heart began thudding in a ridiculous manner when I saw Alan getting out of his car in the drive.

"Hullo!" I called, pulling the pony up.

He fixed me with his brilliant stare. "Good morning," he said coldly, and turned away.

"Alan," I called, and beckoned with my crop, as he glanced round again.

"We don't seem to have met lately," I said feebly, as he came to the gate with obvious reluctance.

"I've been busy," he said shortly.

"And I haven't been altogether idle." I said, smiling. "But you must have some free time. Why don't you come up to the house for a game of tennis sometimes."

"Thank you, I don't play," he replied, with his eyes on Jessup's glossy side.

"Well, come riding. I can find you

a mount," I persisted. His proximity was softening me alarmingly. "Don't be like this, Alan," I pleaded. "I've said I'm sorry."

He looked at me again and cried fiercely: "For God's sake leave me alone." Then he hurried off to the house.

I pulled at Jessup's reins and urged him to a trot and finally, when we had reached a stretch of heathland, to a gallop. Feeling slightly better after that, I rode soberly home.

The old house seemed to glow like a warm and living thing in the sunlight, as I saw it from one particular vantage point, and I pulled the pony up again and sat absorbing the beauty of it. I knew by the goaded tone in which Alan had spoken that my power over him still persisted, even though he meant to resist it. I knew, too, that I was still strongly attracted to him. But what could come of it?

"Nothing," I said aloud. "It's mad to think otherwise."

Jessup gave his head a little shake and I patted his neck and rode on to Westings.

That evening Julian phoned me from New York. His call was no novelty, as he had rung several times since my accident.

"Darling," he said, when he had enquired if I was now fully recovered, "I wish you could be with me here. You'd be a riotous success with all my hostesses, and still more with their husbands. How many men have been trying to make love to you since I went away?"

I hid a feeling of guilt under a light laugh. "Oh scores," I answered. "I've had to think up a special routine to deal with them all."

"The sooner we're married the better, my girl," said Julian. Then, lowering his voice coaxingly, he added: "Let it be soon, Silla."

I had an unpleasant sensation of having been trapped, which was absurd, considering how much, with my saner self, I wanted to be married to my cousin.

"But the engagement isn't even official yet," I said.

"Damn it, darling! We're not discussing a government appointment," said the clear, familiar voice that was coming from so fantastically far away. "You've agreed to marry me, haven't you?"

"Yes," I said, "but — "

"You haven't changed your mind, Silla?" the voice interrupted anxiously.

"No," I said, and repeated more firmly: "No, of course not."

"A slight attack of cold feet?" said the voice. "It'll pass. I wish I could kiss you. You'd soon feel better. Anyway, I'm hustling you to the altar as soon as I get back, so take fair warning."

I was startled by Julian's decisiveness, but I told myself I should be glad of it. It was a lifebelt in the sea of new emotions that were imperilling my plans. This feeling may have given warmth to my voice when I asked: "Are you coming back soon, Julian?"

"Bless you, darling! I wish I could fly back tonight," he answered. "I'd marry you, by special licence, tomorrow. But I can't, worse luck. Our future bread and the thickness of the butter on it, depends a good deal on the state of Judson's Jams and Jellies out here. There are several people I've yet to see."

Afterwards, I went upstairs and took out the sapphire ring and slipped it on my finger. Then I went to my father's study, where he was listening to a broadcast concert, and sat with him quietly till the music came to an end.

"Thank you, my dear," he said, smiling at me. "And how is Julian?"

"Very lively, tonight," I answered, smiling back at him. Then I added seriously: "Daddy, he wants me to marry him quite soon."

"And how do you feel about that?" he asked, looking at me attentively.

"Well, I don't believe in long engagements," I said. "But Julian is talking about a special licence."

"Nonsense!" exclaimed my father. "We'll have nothing rushed, Silla. When you marry it must be with style and dignity. In the village church, with Appleby and your cousin Humphry presiding. A marquee on the lawn by the lake and all the villagers invited, as well as friends and relations. That's how it has always been with the daughters here at Westings."

I couldn't help taking pleasure in the thought.

"If you want a marquee on the lawn, Daddy, we can't have the wedding later than October. We could wait till next spring, of course. But I don't think Julian would be willing," I said.

"I wish your mother were alive," my father remarked wistfully.

I put an arm round his neck and pressed my cheek to his.

"You know you won't be losing me," I said. "Where ever Julian and I decide to live you can be sure it won't be far away, and I shall always be coming back to Westings. It will still be my real home. Remember Julian belongs here, too."

"Of course, darling," said my father. "And I intend to be busy again, so that I won't have time to feel lonely when you're away. I'll take up golf and go up to London more often to my club. Join a chess club, too, and get on with the research for the book I mean to write on the William and Mary period in England."

He spoke cheerfully enough, but somehow a slight melancholy descended on us both afterwards.

The very next day Julia, widow of my father's younger brother and mother of Julian, arrived all unheralded. She came in an old and cherished Rolls, driven by her dedicated chauffeur, Clotworthy. She was a small plump woman, still very pretty, with the style and elegance of a certain type of Parisienne. Her mother had been French. She had had everything possible done to her face to keep it youthful and, wisely, nothing at all to her hair. It was naturally loosely curling and prematurely white and it looked like the final triumphant touch of icing sugar on a delicious confection. It was the pride and joy of her Swiss maid, Lucille, who accompanied her almost everywhere, sitting beside Clotworthy like his other half.

"You poor poor child!" she exclaimed, enveloping me in a cloud of ravishing odours as she embraced me.

"What a collection of catastrophes! Jimmy's illness, your accident, and Nanny Price actually going gaga and dosing herself to death. What did you think of my wreath? Perhaps orchids weren't entirely appropriate. But I'm sure she would have loved them."

Julia is the only person I know who calls my father Jimmy.

"You've got thinner, Silla," she continued, standing back a little to look at me. "You need a real holiday from Westings. That's what I've come for. I'm off to Nice tomorrow, and I'm taking you with me."

"But I can't possibly be ready so

129

soon, even if I could go at all," I cried, laughing a little breathlessly.

"Of course you can. What's to stop you?" said my aunt by marriage.

"You know how we're understaffed here," I said. "And now with Nanny gone — "

"Don't pretend *she* was much use," said Julia. "Last time I was here I thought 'housekeeper' was purely a courtesy title for her." She gave a laugh. "Not in the usual sense, of course. Though in the past — But I mustn't bring that up, with the poor old thing so newly dead."

I looked at her in some surprise.

"All I'm saying is, don't make Nanny's death an excuse to make a martyr of yourself," she said.

"Oh dear! I hope I'm not doing that," I said, half-seriously.

"Of course not," said my father. "But it's true, I think, that you need a holiday, darling."

"That's right, Jimmy. Back me up," purred Julia.

"There's really no reason why you shouldn't take advantage of Julia's kind offer. Friedrich and Mrs. Dean can manage well enough, with Mrs. Welsh and Conny to help them," he ended.

"But tomorrow!" I cried. "What about clothes?"

"Evening dresses and beach-wear are the important things, and we can buy the beach-wear out there."

If riches can't work miracles they can, sometimes, bring the improbable to pass, and I was still feeling slightly incredulous, as I sat in the aircraft next day gazing out at a floor of soft white cloud that looked substantial enough to hold a whole company of fat white cherubim.

When I got home, I reflected, Julian would probably be back too. Then there would be all the fuss about our engagement and all the social activities that would mean. After that would come preparations for the wedding and the search for a suitable house. It should be easy to avoid Alan Laird.

I had a painful notion that it would be all the easier because he would be doing his best to avoid me. I wondered what had possessed him to practically propose to me in the garden of Westings on the evening of our small dinner party. It was clear that I no more fitted into any plans he might have for his future than he did into mine. He would probably marry Sylvia Paul and be quite happy after all. I might have been entirely wrong in my judgement of her character. Jealousy gives one a bias, and I admitted to myself I had felt a strong pang of jealousy when I had first heard of Alan's interest in her. The memory still hurt, but the pain would pass.

Surprisingly soon we were at the big white hotel and I was gazing out across a dazzling foreground of geraniums at palm trees and a sea that — today at least — was as blue as picture postcards would have the Mediterranean.

For three weeks I lived a life that was entirely different from my normal one. I even seemed to myself, at times, to be a different person. There were plenty of young people staying at our hotel or neighbouring ones, many of them my aunt's acquaintances. Mixing with them I lost the feeling I sometimes had of not quite belonging to my own generation. With them I swam and sunbathed and played and drove about, and afterwards, though half-bewildered with light and heat and air and water, still had enough energy to dance half the night away.

Julia was pleased to see me enjoying my youth, as she put it. Apparently she had no misgivings when young men were attracted to me and I made companions of them, not even over Georgio an Italian boy with a smooth olive skin and melting dark eyes who showed an ardent desire to be with me at all times — even after I had gone to bed, though I dealt firmly with that.

All the time, in the background of my consciousness was the knowledge that Westings waited serenely for its mistress's return and that the steady reliable support of my father's love was there to go back to also. We exchanged letters by airmail and I had one or two brief telephone conversations with him, at Julia's expense, and he reported that all was well at home.

I sent postcards to Friedrich and Mrs. Dean and to a few of the local people who had known me since I was a child, and I posted cards to the young Prices too. Looking back it seems strange how little I thought about those two, especially considering a conversation I had had with Julia concerning them, before we left.

She had been curious to see Nanny's grandchildren and when, for some reason or other, they had come up to the house I introduced them and at the same time told them that she was whirling me off to the South of France almost immediately.

"What luck!" exclaimed Adrian, who was looking his most handsome. "Now you won't be able to be a witness at my trial." He was referring to his coming appearance at our local magistrates' court to answer to a summons for dangerous driving. He and I had slipped into a way of joking about that disastrous first meeting of ours. It saved embarrassment under the circumstances.

"Oh Silla, how I envy you!" cried Letta. "I wish I was going too." She put on a pathetic little girl act. "But I haven't got no fairy Godmuvver meself."

Afterwards Julia, who had been most gracious to them, said: "I should watch that young man, my dear. He has more charm than is good for him. The girl's very attractive too. Of course the grandmother was reputed to be a beauty in her day. That's what caused the scandal leading to William Price hanging himself. But he must have been very unbalanced to do such a thing, and if the story had been true one would have thought Nanny would have exploited the situation a little.

She always does seem to have had a rather privileged position in the family, though, doesn't she."

"Dr. Robbie mentioned the affair to me the other day," I said. "It was the first time I really heard what poor William's grudge against the family was supposed to be."

The memory of what I had fancied I had seen from Nanny's window came chillingly into my mind, but I pushed it away.

"What I can't understand is why he should have committed suicide after so long a lapse of time. Charles was dead and the marriage must have been more or less secure by then."

"Why, the story is that he had only just discovered that Nanny's son, whom he was terribly proud of and devoted to, wasn't his child at all, but your great uncle's," said Julia.

"Oh, so that was it!" I exclaimed.

"Mind, there was no proof whatever," said Julia firmly. "All the gossips had to go upon was Charles's reputation with women, which wasn't good, his opportunity and the fact that Nanny married William in a hurry a few weeks after Charles went off to America, where he was soon afterwards killed. When she had a child seven months after the wedding, of course people talked a bit more, but William didn't seem to have heard the rumours till some years later."

"Then it's just possible that Adrian and Letta are my cousins," I said wonderingly.

"Second cousins," Julia corrected me, rather pedantically. "They would be your father's first cousins once removed. But, as I said, it's all very unsubstantiated. Your Uncle Howard told me all he knew about it, but, of course, he never knew what was the truth. Only Nanny knew that, and *she* won't talk now."

It might have been my fancy that, though Julia added a conventional "Poor soul!" there was a note of satisfaction in her voice.

This conversation had an effect upon me at the time, making me think about the young Prices with fresh interest, but away from England and in my holiday surroundings, other things soon pushed it to the back of my mind.

Then, in the midst of my carefree existence, I received a jolt. A letter arrived for me from Mary Peach.

7

WE had driven to San Remo with Georgio, in his white Mercedes and had been eating ices at a table outside a gay little restaurant. Georgio had taken Julia off to find a certain shop and I was feeling lazy and had decided to sit where I was and wait for their return. Then I remembered the letter, which I had slipped into my handbag unread in the hurry of our leaving the hotel. I took it out and opened it.

"My dear Drusilla," I read. "I'm not sure whether I am really doing the right thing in sending you this letter, but I know you will believe that I am actuated only by feelings of friendship for yourself and Sir James and concern for the well-being of both of you. I have a feeling that your father has serious need of you. I think there is something worrying him and making him seem unlike himself. I know how close you and he are to each other and can imagine how he misses having you to confide in, but, knowing how unselfish he is where you are concerned, I can also imagine how he hesitates to spoil your holiday. I am sorry I cannot be more explicit. I have only this deep sense that something is very wrong at Westings. Yours very sincerely and affectionately, Mary Peach."

Alarm and guilt struck me. I suddenly felt that I was in an alien and unfriendly place, a long way from the home I loved. The white glare of the sky seemed heartless, the shimmering dance of light on the sea, the flowers, the bright awnings and colourful clothes seemed to mock me. When I saw Julia and Georgio strolling back towards me in the sunshine, smiling and talking, I felt impatient with them for not hurrying. I put the letter back in my handbag and rose and joined them quickly.

"Julia," I said abruptly: "How soon can I get home?"

"Back to the hotel?" said my aunt, looking surprised.

"Back to England," I said.

"To England." said my aunt, as though this was a country she had vaguely heard of but never visited.

"I had a letter today," I explained. "I read it only just now. Daddy needs me at Westings. He's not well."

"Does he say so?" asked Julia, frowning, while Georgio's eloquent eyes expressed alarm and sympathy.

"Not exactly," I answered, not wishing to betray what I felt to be a confidence. "But I can tell."

"There's something I must say to you, Silla," said my aunt, walking, at too fast a pace to be pleasant in that temperature, to where we had left the car. "Ever since your mother died you have been trying to be responsible for your father as well as for the running of Westings. But Jimmy is responsible for himself, and has been for years before

141

you were born. Whatever will you do after you are married?"

"I shall go to him whenever I think he needs me," I said. "Julian will understand."

"I shouldn't count too much on that," said Julian's mother dryly.

Georgio was looking from one to the other of us, he felt in his pocket for his car-keys. Now he stopped and said tragically! "Silla is to marry? Oh no!"

"Oh yes," snapped my aunt.

"To this man, Julian?" continued Georgio, scowling. "Then I will kill him."

"He happens to be my son," said Julia.

"Your son!" Georgio appeared to be wrestling with himself. "For your sake I will let him live," he said, with obvious appreciation of his own nobility of character.

"Thank you. That's big of you," said Julia, who seemed very put out.

"Of course, I don't want to spoil your holiday, Julia," I said placatingly.

"You've been wonderfully kind and I'm very grateful for the marvellous time you've given me. But you've got lots of friends and you wouldn't be lonely out here if I left you now."

"I will see that the Signora is never lonely," Georgio promised, as he opened the car door with a flourish.

I said I was sure he would. As a matter of fact, with the Latin appreciation of an attractive woman irrespective of her age, he had been showing Julia almost as much attention as he paid to me. I suspected him of having hopes — quite unjustified I'm sure — that the widowed Signora would have more liberal views on love than a young girl like myself and would be prepared to put them into practice, too.

"You may have to wait for a seat on a plane," said my aunt, in a tone that told me she had accepted the situation. "Unless there's a cancellation."

As it happened, there was, and I was in the air and bound for London that very afternoon. Georgio drove me to the airport, and Julia accompanied us, looking very chic in a dress of apricot coloured silk, long black gloves and a big black hat. The sight of her seemed to give Georgio some consolation when he said good-bye to me.

Half an hour after I had left the ground my three weeks of sunshine and sea and fun and leisure seemed no more than a dream. I was on my way back to my real life and the things that really mattered, Westings and my father's companionship. I was worried about him, of course, but I couldn't feel unhappy, because I was going home.

We flew into cloud over the channel and landed in a fine drizzle. The air felt soft and cool after the heat of the Riviera and I was glad to put on the light coat I carried. I had only small hand-luggage with me and was having the rest sent on, which meant less delay at the airport.

I had intended phoning my father as

soon as I got to the terminal, but there was no telephone immediately available and I was afraid of missing my train. So I left it, thinking my father's pleasure might be all the greater if I took him by surprise.

I felt as if I had been travelling all day, but it was still only eight o'clock when I arrived at our local station, I call it local, but it was some five miles from Westings itself.

The porter taking the tickets of the few passengers who alighted there was Alfred Welsh, husband of one of our daily maids. He touched his cap to me and smiled, then took a peep out into the road.

"The car's not here yet, Miss D'alquen," he said helpfully.

"I'm not expecting to be met, Mr. Welsh," I told him. "I want a taxi."

He shook his head and stuck out his moustached upper lip. "I don't know as you'll be lucky there, miss," he said. "Jo Smiley would have obliged, I'm sure, but he's taken the Missis to the pictures." Then his gaze went past me and he gave a grunt. Stepping outside he whistled shrilly.

I saw that Alan Laird had just come out of a tobacconists opposite, and was walking towards his car parked at the kerb.

He glanced across and saw me and our gazes locked. The sensible decisions I had come to concerning him suddenly seemed meaningless. I felt my heartbeats quicken.

"Doctor!" yelled Alfred Welsh. Then, as Alan came towards us he explained: "I thought if you was going home you might like to give Miss D'alquen a lift."

"Of course," said Alan, with stiff politeness and murmured a greeting to me.

I was feeling half-annoyed at the porter's officiousness, but he had obviously meant to be kind and felt a kind of proprietorship in me. So I thanked him and walked in silence to Alan's car.

"I've come home on impulse," I explained as he opened the door for me. "So nobody is expecting me."

"I see." He gave me a longer glance. "You're looking well." He sounded as if he had been about to say something slightly different but had thought better of it.

"Thank you," I said, beginning to enjoy this chance companionship. "But do you know how my father is?" I asked quickly. "Have you seen him lately?"

"No," be answered, getting in beside me.

"Has Dr. Robbie?" I asked anxiously.

He started the engine before he answered me. "Not professionally, if that's what you mean," he said.

I leaned back with a little sigh. So it wasn't my father's health that was the trouble — unless it was something he wished to keep secret from his doctor. But that would be out of character. Could he be in financial deep waters? If it was anything that put Westings in danger I could certainly imagine it causing anxiety to my father. Then I decided not to speculate. Once I was home I would soon find out what was wrong.

Alan was a good and careful driver, and I told myself that it was this fact that gave me such a feeling of wellbeing and security, sitting there beside him in the car, with the hood drawn against the drizzle.

"It's good to be coming home," I murmured. "It reminds me of when I was a schoolgirl and had been to the cottage we had at Cornwall. I was always happy to get back to Westings, no matter how much I had enjoyed myself. Only then there was the knowledge that I would have to leave it again soon, to return to school," I added.

"Your home and your father mean a lot to you, don't they," he said quietly.

"Everything," I answered. I used more emphasis than I had intended because of a treacherous little part of my mind that was suddenly sceptical.

"That's an unnatural thing for a girl of your age to say," he said severely, darting a glance at me.

"What you mean, I suppose," I said scathingly, "is that most of your friends couldn't leave home quickly enough, and looked upon their parents as belonging to a different species. Well, perhaps I'm different, and not ashamed of it. I know that I come first with my father."

"That *is* natural," said Alan. "He's a widower and you're his only child."

"*He* comes first with *me*," I said doggedly. "And Westings comes next with both of us."

"Is that why you're going to marry your cousin?" he fired suddenly at me, his face set, his eyes staring straight ahead.

I was silent and shocked.

"I'm sorry. I shouldn't have asked you that," he said, without sounding in the least sorry.

"No," I managed to say, with what dignity I could find. Then shed the dignity and blurted: "How do you know? Did Dr. Robbie tell you?"

"No. It's all over the village," he said. "When you employ some of the villagers inside Westings, you should expect some of your secrets to get out."

Then he gave me a glance of sheer unhappy reproach. "You might have told me, that night I made such an exhibition of myself," he said bitterly.

"You didn't give me much chance," I replied.

"Do you love him?" he asked abruptly.

I had a terrible impulse to say: "No, I don't," and add: "I love *you*."

I might have done it, too, if we hadn't been driving along the village street by then and he hadn't stopped to let an old woman cross the road, and the old woman hadn't been a patient and come hobbling up to tell him how much good the new medicine was doing her.

As he drove on again he said: "I shouldn't have asked you that question either."

I had got command of myself and said, rather defensively, perhaps: "I've always been fond of Julian." This was true, as he had been like an elder brother to me in my childhood. "And we have a lot in common, in the things we care for," I finished.

"Such as Westings?" he said dryly.

I didn't answer that. Instead, as we were passing Woodside, I said with cold politeness: "I'm afraid I've taken you out of your way."

"Yes, you have," he said, and I knew that he wasn't referring only to the journey.

I felt a wave of deep unhappiness. "I'm sorry, Alan," I murmured. "I wish — " I broke off.

"Don't apologise," he said harshly. "You can't help being what you are, what you've been made. I'm the one who needs the excuses. I've been a little mad, I think, ever since I saw you coming down that great staircase like — like a picture in a bairn's book."

He put scornful emphasis on the word 'bairn', and I saw suddenly in my mind a little blue-eyed boy, with a rather bulgy forehead, poring entranced over the illustrations to some favourite story.

I wanted to cry, but at this point we reached the main gate of Westings, which was some hundred yards off the motorway, and Alan stopped and got out to open the gate. A little distance within, the lodge — itself looking like the illustration to a fairy-tale — had its door shut fast, its mullioned windows closed. The little stream that ran close to the door babbled along over its invisible bed. The rain was making a rustling like starched skirts in the trees along the avenue.

Alan got in and drove on, and I glimpsed the lake, looking like tarnished silver as it reflected the sky. Then the big rhododendrons blotted out the view, till we came clear of them and swept round to the gravelled space before the house.

The wet seemed to have deepened the rosy glow of its old brickwork, and I looked at it with love and pride, drawing strength from its dear familiar beauty. I was home.

"Good-bye," said Alan, and I found he was holding the car door open for me.

"Good-bye, Alan. And thank you," I said, getting out.

I held out my hand. He barely touched it with his own, but he gave me a look that was momentarily wistful and very disturbing. Then he frowned, as if angry either with himself or me, and got back into the car, turned it with a spouting of gravel from under the wheels and drove away.

Usually I went in and out by the south door of the house, to which I had a key and which opened onto a passage leading to the back staircase. Now, anxious to get in out of the rain, which had become heavier, I went into the pillared porch and rang the bell I heard the dogs bark from within and that increased my sense of homecoming and soothed the disturbance of my feelings still more. After a pause Friedrich opened the door. He stood staring at me so strangely that I laughed. His surprise might almost be taken for consternation, I thought. But that idea was absurd.

"I'm not a ghost, Friedrich," I said, stepping inside and handing him my travelling-bag.

He took it and smiled uncertainly. "No, Miss Silla. I can see you are not," he said with his little bow. "You look most well. But Sir James didn't tell me you were arriving this evening."

"He didn't know," I said. I stooped to pat the dogs and quieten them. "This is a little surprise for him."

I straightened and looked round the hall as I had done when I had returned from my short stay in hospital. I noticed at once that this time there were changes. The big

Chesterfield had been pulled round to face in a different direction. A Chinese bowl that belonged to the garden room stood on an inlaid table from the drawing-room. It was full of late flowering August roses. A rococo mirror that usually hung in one of the shut-up rooms upstairs had replaced the riotous still-life by a pupil of Pieter de Ring above the fireplace.

"Why Friedrich!" I said, staring.

"Yes, there are changes, Miss Silla," he said quietly. "But all the time, everywhere, this is happening." He looked into my eyes and continued: "Even in people. Most of all, I think sometimes in people. The blood, the bones, the mind. All the time they change. It is some thing to be accepted."

This philosophising was so odd that I knew he was trying to prepare me for something. I was alarmed again.

"My father!" I said, with the alarm turning to terror. "He isn't — there's nothing wrong with him, is there?"

"No no. He is well," answered Friedrich loudly.

Then the door beyond the staircase opened and my father came through. He checked himself and exclaimed when he saw me, then came forward eagerly.

"Silla! My dear child! This is very unexpected," he said, and took me by the shoulders and kissed me tenderly. I was so delighted to see him, and so relieved that I giggled like a schoolgirl who has played a successful prank. My father stood back and looked at me and I caught a glimpse, then, of the same sort of expression that had been in Friedrich's eyes, anxiety mingled with calculation.

"You couldn't have got my letter already!" he said. "No, of course not. I only posted it yesterday evening."

"No," I said. "But I suddenly felt terribly homesick and made up my mind to come home all in a moment. Luckily there was a seat on a plane available, so here I am."

I spoke gaily, but I was uneasy, and, before I had finished, my gaze had been held by a shadow beyond the doorway through which my father had entered. was somebody hovering there?

The shadow moved and became a girl in a black sleeveless dress. Of course. It was Letta. Her bright hair was piled up on top of her small head. Diamonds glittered in her ears. She looked very very pretty.

"Darling!" she exclaimed. "This is a surprise!"

Then, to my astonishment, she came forward and took my father's arm in a familiar way, and smiled and licked her lips. I think now that she was nervous, but I thought then she looked like a cat that has been in the larder during the housewife's absence.

"Isn't it a marvellous surprise, Jimmy?" she said, with a sweet glance up at him.

I stared as if I was in one of those horrible dreams where one can't move a muscle to save one's life.

"But we have a surprise for Silla, too, haven't we darling?" purred Letta.

"Silla, my dear," said my father quietly, looking at me with both pity and appeal in his fine eyes. "I'll tell you now what was in my letter to you. I hope you'll understand and wish us well. Yesterday Letta and I were married — very quietly — by special licence."

8

IT was fantastic nonsense! It couldn't be true. I looked from my white-haired, sixty-eight year old father to the near stranger at his side, the girl who, even if she appeared younger than her age, couldn't be more than twenty-eight and was probably less than twenty-five. Then I looked into their eyes and knew that it was true. I put out my hands as if to keep off something unclean, and backed away.

"No!" I said. I don't know now whether I whispered it or shouted it, but I know there was more than incredulity in that little word. There was utter rejection.

"Silla!" said my father and would have stepped forward, but Letta clung to his arm as if to stop him.

"I said it would be a surprise to you, Silla," she said quickly. "Poor darling!

You look quite stunned. I expect you're tired, too, after that ghastly journey. And have you had dinner? Oh dear! I don't believe you have. I'll ring for Friedrich and see what there is."

I don't know whether it was the tone in which she said: "Poor darling," or her natural seeming assumption of the role of mistress of the house that made me pull myself together. I must not make an exhibition of my outraged feelings before her. To help me, a hard and stony anger began to take shape within me. I would not look again at my father's troubled face.

"I'm not hungry, thank you," I said coldly. "But I am very tired. If you don't mind I'll go straight to my room."

Then, as if they were acquaintances to whom I was obliged by good manners to be polite, I said: "Do accept my congratulations. I hope you'll both be very happy." But the bitterness would not be entirely denied, and I added: "Stranger things have

160

happened." And I walked past them and up the stairs with a steady step and my head erect.

But when I was in my own pretty room, with the door safely locked, I found that I was shaking all over. I sat down on the bed and pulled the puffy white eiderdown round me. The cold anger was still with me, but so was a terrible sense of loss and betrayal and disillusionment. I felt a kind of sick wonder and astonishment, too. What had possessed my father to do this thing? It seemed entirely out of character. I thought of his integrity, fastidiousness and pride of race, that was always tempered with good sense. I even wondered if his mind could have become affected in some way, and remembered the illness that had made him give up his public activities some years before. I had been away at school at the time and had never been told much about it.

Then I saw again the expression on my father's face and I told myself he had known exactly what he had done. Was he no different, then, from any other vain, sensual, foolish elderly man who hankered after a girl-bride? I couldn't bear to think that. Had he married Letta as an insurance against loneliness? Perhaps my absence had given him a taste of what life would be like for him at Westings after my marriage. But there was Mary Peach. No stranger, obviously devoted, near to his own age and far more suitable by background and breeding to be his wife. Why hadn't he married her?

All the time I had been pushing away another possible explanation. Now I deliberately considered it, though it brought additional pain with it. I remembered the rumour I had heard, that my father had married his second wife, my mother, chiefly to get an heir. Suppose he had noticed how much Alan Laird attracted me and was afraid that my engagement to Julian might be broken off. Could he possibly be hoping for a new, direct heir, another son? Was it likely, at his age? What was it I had said with such painful irony just now? Stranger things had happened.

I didn't ask myself what Letta's motives were in marrying my father. I had no doubt that I knew. She had married for security and position, of course, to be Lady D'alquen and the mistress of Westings. Surely my father, who had never been a great self-deceiver, must suspect this, at least. But perhaps he didn't care.

It was then that I suddenly had a moment of self doubt.

I had felt nothing but contempt for what I had imagined were Letta's motives in this marriage. But weren't my own reasons for wanting to marry Julian much the same? Only I would have put the last motive first. To be the mistress of Westings. And if my father had married with the idea of producing a son who could inherit the place, weren't my own intentions much the same as his, too?

I was temporarily shaken out of my mood of bitter condemnation. But only very briefly. Of course I told myself that my case was quite different. That Julian and I were well matched in age, upbringing and interests. That we knew each other well, yes, and loved each other, even if it wasn't speaking for myself in a romantic and exciting way.

I started as a tapping sounded at the door, and sat up rigid and tense. Could it be my father, or Letta? I kept very still and remained silent.

Then the tapping came again and the handle was gently turned.

"Miss Silla," said Friedrich's voice. "Please open the door. I have brought food for you. You must eat, Miss Silla, or you will be ill."

I had a childish thought that this would be a good thing and would serve my father right. Then I was ashamed, and got up, throwing down the eiderdown, and went to the door and opened it.

Friedrich's lined face was anxious, as he limped in with the tray and set it on a small table and drew up a white bedroom chair.

"You must eat it at once, Miss Silla," he said. "See, it is a mushroom omelette, with thin brown bread and butter and some salad. Mrs. Dean had not gone home and she said 'I will not give Miss Silla my left-overs. I should be ashamed. I shall make her a nice omelette'. And here is cheese and biscuits and I have brought a glass of Beaujolais and a little brandy. It is a good tonic, brandy."

I felt my eyes fill with tears. I knew that Friedrich was telling me discreetly that the members of Westings' domestic staff were on my side, that I had all their sympathy.

"Thank you both," I said, sitting down and unfolding my napkin, though my throat seemed to close at the sight of food.

The tray was daintily laid, as if for an invalid, and had a yellow rose in a tiny cut-glass vase on it.

Friedrich gave his little bow in acknowledgement of my thanks. There was so much I wanted to ask him. What had happened from the beginning between my father and Letta, once I was away? Had she set out deliberately to capture him? Had my father made the first moves? Had they been open or secretive about their budding relationship? Friedrich was an old friend, as well as an employee, and there was affection and understanding in his eyes. But pride and loyalty both forbade my discussing my father with him.

I said simply: "You were right to warn me about changes, Friedrich."

"Yes," he said sadly. "I was right. But this, too will pass. Nothing is permanent, Miss Silla."

"There's something rather permanent about marriage, even in these days," I said, trying to smile.

But he shook his head and repeated: "Nothing is permanent." Then he added: "Except perhaps death."

I sensed that this was a philosophy that had supported him at a time of suffering I couldn't even imagine. It was one that did not appeal to my youth and egoism, however. "Well, nobody's going to die," I said rather irritably.

"Everybody is going to die sooner or later," he answered. "Please ring for coffee, Miss."

I ate and drank as much as I could. The brandy helped a little. Friedrich shook his head over the debris on the tray when he carried it away.

"In the morning you will feel better, Miss Silla," he said kindly. "You think you will not sleep, but you will. Always the young can sleep."

I didn't believe him, and wondered how I was to get through the night. I unpacked the little I had brought back with me and took a bath and sat before the mirror brushing my hair like an automaton, bemused with shock and misery. I got into bed and lay back against the pillows and closed my eyes and at once my mind seemed to whir with activity.

I had locked the door again and presently there came a tapping that was quite different from Friedrich's. I knew who was there before he spoke, and I kept very still and silent.

"Silla," said my father's voice very softly. "Silla, my darling, won't you speak to me?"

There was a tenderness in his tone that nearly broke me, but I hardened my heart and refused to respond, and presently he went away. I wept then as I had not wept since my mother's death, and at last I fell asleep exhausted.

I woke early and for one moment of wonderful relief, thought my father's marriage to Letta an absurd dream. Then reality burst in, bringing renewed unhappiness. How was I going to face the pair today? Could I possibly bear to see Letta coming first with my father, Letta mistress of Westings in my place? I answered these questions promptly. I couldn't, of course. I must leave as soon as possible. But at the thought of relinquishing my adored home another pang of anguish shook me.

I thought of flying back to Nice at once, as a temporary measure. But I had overspent while on holiday. I had a small income from some investments left to me by my mother and my father made me an adequate allowance. But I couldn't expect any payment from either source for a week at least, and certainly wasn't going to ask my father to advance me any money now. Besides, I could imagine that Julia would come rushing back to England when she heard my news, saying that her brother-in-law must have gone mad.

I thought of Julian. Why wasn't he here, instead of in the States, at this crisis in my affairs? He could provide a dignified way of leaving Westings. The way of speedy marriage. I saw myself a bride, standing before the altar of the village church, just as I had imagined it, when my father and I had discussed my wedding. Only the man at my side wasn't my cousin Julian, it was Alan Laird.

But this was nonsense, I told myself. I had settled all that. Alan despised me now and regretted what he called his madness in allowing himself to be attracted by me. I writhed inwardly when I thought how I had boasted to him of the deep understanding and trust between my father and myself and our mutual devotion to Westings. Had he known what was in store for me and laughed up his sleeve?

But I dismissed the idea at once. He had not known, or he would have said. Neither had Mary Peach known. I was convinced of that. She was not a devious person. She implied, in her letter, that she was afraid my father was suffering from some unidentified strain. I could believe that this was so. He must have known considerable mental conflict before taking the step he had.

It was a bright clear morning after the night of rain. Sweet country scents, cool and very English, came through my window, contrasting with the warm airs of my holiday mornings. I decided to get up and go for a ride. In the past I had often taken my problems and grief — very minor ones they seemed to me now for a canter, and found them diminish.

There was a strange black horse in the stable-yard, and a strange, black-clad man holding its bridle. The sight was a fresh shock to my nerves. Then I saw that the man was Adrian Price. I had not recognised him at once because he had let his hair grow longer during my absence and had cultivated a small curly beard. Seeing him like that I realised suddenly why I had experienced that sense of having seen him before, at some time earlier than our actual meeting. It was not because of any television appearance. It was because he was like my great-grandfather. The resemblance was much clearer now. He reminded me of a portrait of this ancestor that hung in the dining-room.

There was a family joke that it was the work of Landseer, so lovingly had the unknown artist dealt with the curly black hair and beard of his sitter.

Could it be true then, that he and I — and Letta too — were of the same blood?

His face had brightened most disarmingly at the sight of me.

"Silla, darling, you're back!" he exclaimed, while I was still feeling confused and taken aback, by the revelation of his changed appearance. "How ravishing you look with all that gorgeous tan! How was Nice? And when did you get home?"

"Nice was hot. And I flew back yesterday," I said.

He gave me a shrewd look. "And found you had a young stepmother," he said. "Weren't you completely shattered?"

I was so startled by this frankness that I was not able to find a suitable reply immediately, and he didn't wait for one.

"I was quite knocked over myself when Letta sprang it on me," he continued. "I mean, there is a terrific difference in their ages, isn't there!"

"There are other differences too," I said dryly, recovering my poise.

"You're thinking of background and education and all that," said Adrian, apparently quite unoffended. "Ye-es. But Letta's awfully adaptable, you know. An actress has to be. Marriage is strange, isn't it! Couples get hitched and make a do of it that you'd never dream had a thing in common. I think it was all that old-world charm and distinction that attracted my sister to your father."

He gave me another shrewd look. "I'm not saying she wasn't a bit sold on the idea of being Lady D'alquen and mistress of all this." He waved a graceful hand round him.

"And my father?" I said challengingly. "What was his inducement?"

"We-ell," he said, patting his horse, which was becoming slightly restive.

"You're in a better position to tell me that. I don't know Sir James awfully well."

"Do I?" I felt like asking. But I didn't, of course. Instead I said with unconcealed bitterness: "I notice you don't call him Jimmy."

"Should I?" he asked with an air of innocence, glancing round again. He continued: "Of course it's going to be rather difficult for Letta at first. But perhaps, when the situation has settled down a bit, you could help her, Silla."

"Help her?" I repeated incredulously.

He faced me again. "Oh, I expect you hate her guts at the moment," he said crudely, with a wry grin. "But Letta's a frightfully good-natured type you know. She's really very sweet, though I say it who shouldn't. And she admires you, and actually wishes she were like you. She told me that when we first met you. She'd take advice and guidance from you."

I was no more proof against flattery

than most people, and his odd mixture of devastating frankness and tact had softened my attitude a little already. So had my discovery of his resemblance to my great-grandfather. I was convinced now that he and Letta were D'alquens, even though of illegitimate descent. Somehow this made me feel less bitter towards Letta, though my father's behaviour still seemed outrageous to me.

"All right, Larry. All right, boy," said Adrian, addressing the discontented horse. "I hope you don't mind my stabling him here," he said. "Sir James said you wouldn't."

"There's room, certainly," I said rather ungraciously, going in to Jessup, who had been whinnying impatiently.

"I say," called Adrian, who was now mounted. "Would you mind awfully if I rode with you? I'm still a new boy here, and you know all the best rides."

It was difficult to refuse him. I agreed, again rather ungraciously. It was still quite early, and there were few people about as we went through the village, but Alan's car came nosing through the gateway of Woodside, with Alan himself at the wheel. He looked startled at sight of us. Adrian waved gaily.

"Poor devil!" he said as we rode on. "Called out to a hatching or a dispatching, I suppose, or some grisly sick-bed. What a life! Can you imagine that I actually thought Letta was starting to fancy herself as a doctor's wife, soon after we first came here?"

"What?" I exclaimed, with a horrible feeling that some new, unpleasant revelation was coming.

He laughed. "Oh, it wasn't serious, as it turned out. But she seemed to find our rugged Dr. Kildare very fascinating for a time. He's that Puritan type that does have its attraction for somebody like my sister. You know. Hints of banked up fires about him, and volcanoes of passion liable to erupt at any moment."

I felt myself becoming warm. "What nonsense!" I exclaimed. "Alan Laird is a perfectly normal ordinary man."

He laughed again. "That's what Letta found out, apparently."

I badly wanted to question him, for it was new — and disturbing news too — that his sister and Alan were more than the merest acquaintances.

I said: "I thought Letta scarcely knew Dr. Laird."

"She consulted him about some trifle," said Alan. "And made sure she wasn't cured too speedily," he added with amusement. "But, as I said, it wasn't serious. Not on her part, at any rate? Can we take this bridleway? It looks as if it might lead somewhere interesting."

Again I wanted to question him. What had he meant by saying 'Not on her part at any rate', in just the way he had? As if he half-suspected Alan of being seriously interested in his sister.

And why shouldn't Alan have been? I

asked myself that, as we cantered across the Heath. I myself had made it clear I didn't want him. Letta had been free then. Alan had a perfect right to have as many girl-friends as he chose. But it was only my reason that subscribed to this view. Emotions and instincts were deeply against it.

At least, I had stopped thinking exclusively of my father's marriage, and perhaps I should have been grateful to Adrian for that. When we were riding side by side again, he told me that he was growing the beard for a small part in a film.

"Not that it's absolutely in the bag yet," he said cheerfully. "And if I do get the part most of my scenes will probably be cut shockingly. One expects that. But it will help me to eat."

"Is it to be set in Victorian times?" I asked, glancing at him to see if he understood the reference.

He gave no sign of doing so. "Good gracious no," he said. "It's to be just another go at those ghastly Merry Men of Sherwood. Robin Hood and all that, you know."

When we got back to Westings, Adrian invited me to have breakfast with him at the lodge.

"I can cook an egg as well as the next man," he boasted. "And my instant coffee is the best money can buy. I always burn the toast, but *you* can make that."

I was tempted for a moment. His light-heartedness had its appeal, and there was the link I believed to be between us of shared blood as well as his indirect involvement in my father's strange marriage. All these things made his company more acceptable than most at that time. But I couldn't put off my next meeting with Letta and my father indefinitely. Better get it over as soon as possible.

As I went indoors my kitten, Angelique appeared, from the direction of the kitchen. I gave a little cry of pleasure and greeting. But she was so young that my three weeks absence had made me almost a stranger again, and she backed away then turned and ran. Ridiculously, this added to my sense of hurt betrayal, and I went to breakfast in a mood of desolation.

My father was alone at the table. We looked at each other warily. I said nothing and made no move towards him. He rose and came to me and put his hands on my shoulders and kissed my cheek.

"We shall be *tête-à-tête* as usual, my dear," he said quietly. "Letta isn't an early riser, apparently."

"Actresses aren't, I believe," I said as I sat down. I spoke quite coolly, but my heart was hammering away. I looked at the *Telegraph* and began eating grapefruit. My father picked up his copy of *The Times*. But we were neither of us reading. Suddenly my father put the paper down.

"Silla," he said earnestly, "don't let this marriage of mine come between us. Believe me, it can make no possible difference to my love for you."

I wanted so much to believe him. But how could I? Why had he married in such haste, almost stealthily, and without giving me the slightest warning of his intentions? The letter he spoke of must have been written only at the last minute. The recollection hardened me again.

"I've just thought of something rather funny," I said. "If Nanny had lived she would have been your grandmother-in-law," and I laughed derisively.

"Nanny is dead," he answered gravely. "I'm not — yet. And it's my relationship with you — our very real relationship — we're discussing now."

I was ashamed now and I let my natural feelings show. "Oh Daddy, how could you have done it!" I cried wretchedly.

He gave me the strangest look. "One day, darling, perhaps you'll understand," he said.

And then Friedrich entered, and our privacy was gone.

But although my unhappiness and bewilderment persisted, my bitterness was over, because I felt that my father had spoken the truth. His love for me was unchanged, in spite of all appearances. I hated his marriage, but I knew that I still loved him and I couldn't exactly hate his new wife. I decided, in the course of the day, that Adrian was right about his sister. She was good-natured, and she did seem anxious for my friendship and help. My father shut himself in the room which was part study and part library just as usual, after breakfast, and when Letta did at last emerge from the bedroom that had been my mother's, she looked rather forlorn, I thought.

Oddly enough, I had no particular feeling about her using that room. It seemed just a small part of the whole revolting situation to me. It did cross my mind that she probably wouldn't find it really to her taste.

She found me, by force of habit,

arranging the flowers Benson had belatedly brought in and tackled me at once.

"Oh Silla, darling, don't be cross with me," she pleaded. "I just couldn't say no when your father asked me to marry him, because he is such an absolute poppet and I do love him. And you will speak to the servants for me, won't you? They're all stuffy with me. And do, please, just carry on as usual."

I looked at her doubtfully, but her face had an expression of childish appeal.

"All right. For the time being. If that's how you want it," I said curtly.

But I knew that she would soon gain in confidence and experience and would want to be mistress of Westings in fact, as well as in name. When that happened it would be time for me to go, no matter how hard the wrench would be.

Late that afternoon Julian telephoned. "Hello, darling. Guess where I am," he said gaily as soon as I had greeted him.

"In England," I answered promptly, for there had been none of the preliminaries of a transatlantic call.

"You win the jackpot," he said. "I'm at London Airport. Get out that sapphire ring and put on your very best smile, because I'll be with you at Westings just as soon as I can make it."

9

"JULIAN," I said quickly, for I was afraid he would ring off. "There's something I've got to tell you, at once, to prepare you."

"Bad news? Is Uncle James ill?" he asked with concern.

"No," I answered. "Nobody's ill."

"Oh. Well, bad news keeps. Won't this wait till we meet, Silla?" he said, sounding wary and rather uneasy, as if he had an idea of what I was going to tell him. But, of course, he couldn't have had a notion.

"Daddy has married again," I told him flatly.

"What?" He was astonished, but relieved too. "Good for him!" he exclaimed with a laugh. "I suppose Miss Peach is the lady?"

"No," I said. Then I began to wonder just how private our conversation was, for I had heard a faint click, as though somebody had lifted the receiver of one of the extensions in the house. But I continued: "She's an actress, and Daddy has known her for about two months. She's not much older than I am, if at all. Her name is Violet Price, she's known as Letta and she's old Nanny Price's granddaughter."

After a brief blank silence, Julian said: "You're joking." But I could tell by his tone that he knew I was not.

"I don't think I ever felt less like joking in my life," I answered, and my voice quavered slightly.

"Bear up, darling," he murmured sympathetically, then said thoughtfully: "It doesn't sound like your father at all. It certainly is a facer for you. You must tell me all the details later. Good-bye for now, my sweet. Remember I'm on my way."

I listened for, and heard, another faint click before I replaced my own receiver. So the new Lady D'alquen was not above eavesdropping, I thought contemptuously.

I had taken the call in the hall, and as I looked through one of the great windows that gave such a beautiful view of the lake and the gazebo crowned hill beyond, I started, for there by the water was a small figure in the briefest of blue bikinis, bright hair piled on her head and a gaily coloured inflated rubber mattress at her feet. Letta undoubtedly. Then who had been listening in to my telephone talk with Julian?

The daily maids had gone home. Mrs. Dean had arrived to cook dinner. Apart from her there was only Friedrich and my father in the place. It must have been my father, I decided. He had lifted the receiver in his study when the bell had rung. No, it must have been later, for I had heard the click. He had intended to make a call himself. But why hadn't he spoken, when he had heard Julian's voice? Because it would have been too embarrassing in view of the subject we were discussing. But in that case he would have replaced the receiver. He would have thought it dishonourable to go on listening. Then I reminded myself that I could no longer be sure what my father would and would not do.

I went to him in his study. He looked up from an open book as I entered.

"Hullo, my dear," he said easily. "You've come to say tea's ready, I suppose, and I must be sociable. Where's Letta? I hope I haven't been neglecting her too much."

"She's down by the lake," I said. "And, by the way, has she been warned that the water is dangerously deep in places?"

"Oh, I should think so," said my father. "But she wouldn't think of bathing in it, you know. It's obviously none too clean." He sighed. "It used to be periodically drained and cleaned, of course."

But I hadn't come to talk about the lake or our lack of money and staff. "That was Julian on the phone," I said, and looked at him for any signs of embarrassment. But there were none.

"Oh was it?" he said. "Good. And when is he coming home?"

"Now," I said. "He phoned from London. He's on his way here."

"What? Then he should be in time for dinner. That's splendid!" said my father. He appeared genuinely surprised and pleased. "I'm so glad for you, Silla," he remarked softly. "Now your engagement can be made public."

"Yes," I said, looking away from him, out of a window that commanded distant views of trees and a patchwork of fields.

"We must have a party, to celebrate," my father continued. "It will be your occasion, of course, my dear, but — " He appeared to hesitate for a moment. "But it will give our friends and relatives an opportunity of meeting my wife, too."

I left him, feeling consciously defeated. His attitude to Letta was quite baffling. A lovely girl married at impetuous speed, against all sensible considerations, and yet when he spoke of her and when one saw him with her the words 'courteous' and 'dutiful' sprung to the mind. Could it be, I wondered, that he was already regretting, the marriage?

I'm afraid my chief feeling about my cousin's return, was thankfulness that I should now have an ally in my anxiety and my disapproval of Letta's position at Westings. I took it for granted that he would see eye to eye with me in this matter, for our interests were the same. I knew him to be very fond of my father and to have his happiness in mind, as well as being destined to inherit the title and the house.

But when I thought of this, again that uneasy fancy came to me. Suppose — just suppose Letta gave my father a son.

* * *

When Julian arrived, so much had happened to make his time away seem longer than it had actually been that

190

I looked at him with fresh eyes. He was a broad shouldered, rather stocky man, still under thirty, taking after his mother's family in appearance and not the D'alquens. His neat dark head already showed a few grey hairs at the temples, his hazel eyes had a look of alert intelligence behind the thick rimmed glasses.

He kissed me efficiently but not lingeringly. That, I knew, was because of the presence of the smiling Friedrich and my father coming forward with an air of restrained pleasure and guarded dignity. (He guessed, of course, that I had told Julian of his new marriage.) Letta made no appearance till dinner — which had been put back a little — was ready. Adrian had come to the house for luncheon, but had tactfully gone back to the lodge soon afterwards and had not been seen since, so there were just the three of us waiting in the hall with our drinks.

I had been talking with Julian about his experiences in New York, and my father interrupted us to say:

"Letta, my dear, this is my nephew, Julian. Julian, here is my wife."

I turned, and felt a little jolt of surprise. Julian looked at Letta, then glanced briefly at me before going forward politely. I could see that he was surprised, too, for Letta had transformed herself. Normally she used heavy eye make-up. Now she appeared to have none at all. Her bright hair was worn in a Grecian knot. She wore a sleeveless navy-blue dress with a single row of pearls. Altogether she looked almost mouse-like, but it was a very pretty mouse she resembled.

She greeted Julian with an air of shy pleasure.

"How nice to meet you at last," she said softly. "I've heard so much about you. Silla must be wildly excited, I hope you don't mind my knowing about the engagement, but I *am* one of the family now."

"A very charming one too," said Julian, smiling at her.

I had a sudden fear that he was seeing her as a harmless pretty little thing who would probably be a comfort to my father's declining years. I felt frustrated and in the wrong because I wasn't wildly excited by Julian's return.

"Oh thank you," said Letta, giving a wonderful effect of blushing without actually doing so. She spoke as if nobody had ever said a complimentary thing to her before. "I may call you Julian? It seems silly to say Mr. D'alquen when we're related — only by marriage."

There was a queer little silence before Julian murmured: "Of course."

The pause she had made before finishing her sentence made me wonder — not for the first time — if she had any knowledge of real kinship with us D'alquens, and if she shared this with her brother. In such a case I gave them full marks for tact in never mentioning it or making any claim. Or was it discretion rather than tact that kept them silent?

During dinner, my stepmother listened to Julian's account of his social life in the States with an absorbed interest that was, I thought, only partly assumed.

"I've never been to America," she said wistfully. "I had a chance of touring there once, but it fell through. I think New York must be fabulous."

"I prefer Washington," said my father.

"Oh yes. Washington must be marvellous, too," said Letta.

"I haven't been to the States yet, either," I remarked.

"Then how about spending our honeymoon there?" said Julian promptly.

I felt rather annoyed with him for not having made the suggestion to me privately first. And I didn't really want to think about my honeymoon with Julian.

"We'll see," said I, making my lack of enthusiasm obvious.

"You're a lucky, lucky girl to have the chance," cried Letta, who seemed to be shedding the role of shy chatelaine in favour of that of an eager little girl. "I would not hesitate for a moment, in your place." She turned bright, admiring eyes on my cousin.

"Actually I would prefer the Bahamas," I said coldly.

"Then the Bahamas it shall be," said Julian, giving me a swift look of intimacy.

"How simply marvellous to have one's wish gratified just like that!" gushed Letta. She looked across the table at my father. "Jimmy, isn't it marvellous?"

My father, who had been unusually quiet during the meal, said rather dryly: "Julian is a wealthy man. I'm afraid I can't do as much for my wife as he will be able to do for his. I'm sorry my dear."

Letta looked exaggeratedly contrite. "Oh Jimmy darling, you know I wasn't reproaching you. I'm sure you spoil me terribly."

"I do and will continue to do what I can to please you, Letta," said my father with an air of gentle indulgence. "Oh I know, darling," said Letta quickly. Then she gave him an odd glance and licked her lips and toyed with her wineglass as if she were suddenly nervous. "As a matter of fact there is one thing I want done that wouldn't cost anything. Benson could do it, with some help from the boy and Adrian."

"What's that? Make a new flower-bed for you somewhere?" said my father, smiling slightly.

"No. Cut down that ghastly old tree," said Letta. And for a moment she looked tense and adult and almost plain.

"What tree is that?" asked my father, kind but obtuse.

"The big dark one near the house that — that has the horrible story about it," said Letta.

"The old cedar?" said my father and Julian together, each in a tone of incredulity.

I had known instantly which tree

she meant, remembering her fear and horror in Nanny Price's room when she and her brother had come to look over her grandmother's things.

"I can't possibly have that tree cut down, my dear," said my father, as if he were reasoning with a foolish child. "It's over two hundred years old."

"It's a kind of heirloom," said Julian smiling.

"It's part of the history of Westings," I told her.

"Well, it's a bloody unpleasant part," snapped Letta, with an unexpected flash of temper. The small hand that held the wineglass trembled. "I should have thought you would have been damned glad to get rid of it."

I stared at her, knowing that this moment I was seeing the natural Letta, and finding it oddly disturbing.

"You don't understand, I'm afraid," said my father patiently.

Letta glared at him, and his expression changed again. So did her voice and manner. "Oh dear! I'm sorry darling," she said lightly. "I feel awful. As though I had asked you to murder the Archbishop of Canterbury."

Julian laughed.

"Even His Grace would be more easily replaced than our old cedar," said my father, smiling. Then he added soothingly: "You mustn't take any notice of old stories, Letta. Nobody has claimed to have seen poor William's ghost for a long time now, you know."

"Oh that!" said Letta, with a dismissing little shrug. But her hand was still unsteady, and I thought that she breathed rather fast.

I was thinking that my father obviously didn't know about Nanny's alleged ghost — seeing that had alarmed Friedrich, and I had said nothing to him about my own grim fancy, if it was no more than that.

"All the best old houses are haunted, you know," said Julian. "It's the expected thing and enhances their value."

Letta smiled at him, and no more was said about her dislike of the old dark tree.

It was a fine warm night, still and starlit, and Julian and I strolled to and fro on the terrace after dinner, the lights from the house making a twilight there. The scent of the cigar my cousin was smoking blended with the fragrance of the jasmine climbing nearby and the banks of phlox in the garden. Occasionally moths came flitting across our vision and disappeared again into the darkness like tiny ghosts themselves.

"People are full of surprises," said Julian quietly, as I laid my hand lightly on his arm, feeling companionable. "Uncle James and Letta Price! Who could have expected that?"

"What do you really think of her?" I asked him anxiously.

"I think she would be quite a good little actress, if she could make up her mind what role she is supposed to be playing," answered Julian with a little laugh.

I felt a grateful relief. I ought to have known that my shrewd cousin would see through Letta's performances.

Then he astonished me by adding: "I feel sorry for the girl."

"Sorry for her! Why?" I asked.

"Because she's confused and unhappy and I don't think she's really enjoying being mistress of Westings," he answered.

"Then why did she marry Daddy?" I retorted.

"You don't think it's possible she really cares for him?" he said thoughtfully.

I gave something like a snort in reply. "Do you?" I said.

"I suppose not," he murmured. "Though perhaps it's not very complimentary to your father."

"It's not very complimentary to Letta, as I see it," I said.

"No," he agreed, then added: "It's your father's part in the affair I find so perplexing, you know. I wouldn't say *he* showed any signs of being infatuated with *her*, would you?"

"No. He's kind and polite to her, that's all," I said. "Oh, the whole thing has made me absolutely wretched."

He gave my arm a squeeze and patted my hand. "You'll soon be out of it, darling," he murmured. "You're going to marry me. Remember?"

"That won't change anything," I said a little tartly, for it seemed to me he was taking the matter a shade too calmly. "You talk as though you don't really care about what's happened."

He answered carefully: "I'm sorry, of course, that Uncle James has made a fool of himself — if that's what he has done. Otherwise, it doesn't very much concern me, does it?"

I said deliberately, my face flushing in the darkness: "It would concern you, Julian, if Letta gave my father a son."

He was silent and I felt his body tense a little — with surprise, or alarm?

"That's not very likely, is it?" he said slowly at last.

"I don't know," I said. "I suppose it's possible." I think I wanted reassurance more than anything, but he didn't give it.

"Well, there's nothing I can do about it, darling," he told me, with another brief laugh. "Unless you're suggesting that I have your little stepmother liquidated."

"Well," I said, trying to speak as lightly as he had, "there's always the lake handy."

"Now, darling, let's forget Uncle James's love-life and concentrate on our own," he murmured.

He drew me into his arms and kissed me. I thought of Alan's arms and Alan's lips in the July dusk and I wanted to draw back. But I subdued the feeling and tried to respond a little.

The night seemed to have grown darker and chillier, and presently I shivered.

Julian released me with a sigh. "Cold, darling?" he asked.

"Yes. Do you mind if we go in?" I said, and shivered again, this time, I'm afraid, with slight exaggeration.

I was relieved when he went to bed early, excusing himself by saying he was feeling tired after his journey.

I slept only fitfully that night, and during a wakeful spell in the early hours of the morning was appalled to hear a woman's desperate screams coming from somewhere along the corridor.

10

I FLUNG back the sheet and got out of bed with my heart beating fast. I pulled on a nylon wrap, for decency's sake rather than warmth, and opened my door and listened. All was now silent. Then a light sprang up along the wide passage and I saw Julian standing at the other end of it. In his pyjamas, with his hair rumpled and minus his spectacles, he looked surprisingly like the teenage Julian who had bossed and protected me when I was a little girl.

The screams had come, I thought, from my mother's old room, and I went fearfully towards it. Julian came forward, and we met in the middle of the corridor and looked at each other.

"What the hell's going on?" he asked in a low voice.

I shook my head speechlessly, then,

hesitatingly, I rapped with my knuckles on the door.

There was no response.

Julian rapped, more loudly than I had done, and called: "Is there anything wrong?"

We went on staring at each other while we waited, and it seemed quite a long time before the door opened and my father gazed out at us. He was in a dressing-gown of dark blue silk I remember, and he looked pale and rather distraught. Before he spoke, his glance went past us to something beyond. I turned, involuntarily and saw with surprise that Friedrich had joined us. His slippered feet had made no sound on the carpet.

"I beg your pardon, sir," he said, before Julian or I could utter. "I thought I heard somebody cry out. Has there been an accident?"

"No no," replied my father, quite irritably for him. "Lady D'alquen has had nightmare, that's all. You can all go back to bed with easy minds." And he promptly shut the door on us.

Friedrich gave us his little bow and limped silently and imperturbably away. Julian looked at me again and raised his eyebrows.

"Some nightmare!" he murmured. "Our Lady D'alquen sounded more like Lady Macbeth."

I felt my scalp tingle. "What do you mean?" I whispered, drawing him away from the door.

He seemed surprised by my manner. "Why, Letta was an actress, wasn't she? I thought she might have been reliving in dreams some blood curdling part she'd played," he answered.

He put a hand over mine. "I believe you're really frightened," he said softly. "It's all right, you little goose. Go back to bed. Shall I come and tuck you up?"

"No, thanks," I said, dropping his arm, remembering that this was not the old comforting stand-in for elder brother, but a mature man who was in love with me.

I forced a smile, said a hasty good night, and went back to my room, but it was some time before I fell asleep, and then I overslept.

When I went down to breakfast my father and Julian were already sitting over bacon and eggs, cooked by Friedrich. The window was open and the hum of insects mingled with the distant drone of a vacuum-cleaner plied by Mrs. Welsh. Everything seemed normal.

My father greeted me in his usual quietly affectionate manner, and Julian got up, clutching a table-napkin and gave me the kind of kiss a husband of long standing gives his wife when he thinks he may be late for the office.

"I'm sorry I've got to rush away, darling," he said. "But I've been away so long I must show up at the office this morning." He glanced at his watch. "Though I doubt if I'll be there before midday now."

"We've been discussing the announcement of the engagement," my father

207

told me. "I'm sending to *The Times* and the *Telegraph* today."

I had a brief feeling of panic, but I conquered it, nodded and smiled and made a pretence of being hungry.

"And we must start making a list of all the people to be invited to the party," said my father.

"Do we really need to have a party, Daddy?" I asked uneasily. "I'd just as soon go without, you know."

Julian gave me a curious glance.

"Oh, nonsense, darling!" exclaimed my father cheerfully. "It's to celebrate a great occasion. Besides, the family will expect it. And it will give me a chance to show off a little. I am rather proud of my daughter and my nephew."

I was touched, and so, I think, was Julian. I was pleased too, to see him so much like his old self. It was almost as if he had forgotten Letta, till he said: "Of course, Adrian Price must be formally invited, my dear." He turned to Julian. "Adrian is Letta's brother."

"The young man who nearly caused

the death of Silla," said Julian rather grimly. "I shall certainly be interested to meet him."

I had told my cousin of my suspicions concerning the true descent of the young Prices, but he had rather pooh-poohed the idea.

"We must all try to forget that unfortunate accident," said my father quietly. "Adrian has been fined and has had his licence endorsed. I think he will be a better driver in future."

"Let's hope so," said Julian. "It was a good thing Dr. What's-his-name, old Robbie's assistant was on the spot when Silla came to grief," he added.

"Young Laird. Yes. Robbie thinks a lot of him," my father remarked.

To my horror, I felt myself beginning to blush.

"Oh, I shouldn't think he's up to much as a doctor, whatever he's like as a man," said Julian carelessly. "Or he wouldn't be marooned in this part of the world."

The blush was spreading to my neck

now. It was madness to call attention to myself. But I couldn't keep silent.

"Alan Laird is a very good doctor," I declared. "He found out what was wrong with Daddy at once, when Dr. Robbie didn't. And I can think of a lot of reasons why he should have come here."

"Such as what?" asked my cousin, looking amused.

"Lack of a good bedside manner, for one," said my father, with a laugh. "He's one of those downright Scots, isn't he Silla?" He appealed to me quite naturally, without appearing to notice my self-consciousness.

"Well, he does rather tread on toes," I agreed, feeling, with relief, the blush subsiding.

"That was a queer business! Nanny and the digitalis," said Julian abruptly. "Poor old Nanny!"

"Yes, but it was nearly poor Daddy, too," I said soberly. "I've had nightmares about that."

"Speaking of nightmares, I hope

210

Letta has recovered completely from hers," said Julian.

"Thank you. I hope so," said my father, with curious reserve.

"It wasn't anything to do with the old cedar, was it?" asked my cousin. "She certainly seems to have taken a dislike to it."

"No. It doesn't appear to have concerned the cedar," answered my father, passing me his cup for more coffee. He seemed to hesitate before deciding to be more explicit. "She was still only partly awake when I went in to her, but I gathered the dream had been that Nanny had got her on the window-ledge and was trying to push her out of the window, having previously beheaded Adrian." His tone was humorous. "Not the sort of conduct one expects of a grandmother, I admit."

"But Freud would no doubt have an explanation for it," said Julian, grinning. "Something about a guilt complex through being in love with one's grandfather, perhaps. But, of course, Letta never knew poor William Price. If William was her grandfather. Silla seems to think Great Uncle Charles might well have been."

My father appeared to stiffen and the smile left his face abruptly. "Oh?" he said, glancing at me quickly.

I felt absurdly guilty. "It's only that I thought I saw a resemblance between Adrian and Charles's portrait — the Landseer one," I said. "And having heard that old story — "

"I haven't noticed any resemblance," said my father coldly, interrupting. "And some old stories are best forgotten."

Then Friedrich came in to say that a car had arrived for Julian.

"We said the wrong thing just now," murmured Julian to me, as he kissed me goodbye in the hall.

"Yes. I wonder why," I said, feeling drawn to him in the old way, as we exchanged this confidence.

"Honour of the family," answered

Julian, with a shrug and a smile.

But my father was not so old-fashioned as to think his family honour as vulnerable as that. I would have thought, in fact, that he would have welcomed the idea of his bride having D'alquen blood, even unofficially.

Letta came down late, looking wan and listless, and apparently quite content to leave the practical management of the house to me, even to the interviewing of the new housekeeper Mary Peach had found for us during my absence.

Miss Russell startled me at first sight by having dyed black hair and a large bosom, but she had no other resemblance to Nanny Price and her references were excellent. There was a suggestion of 'better days' about her and she won my approval almost at once by her obviously genuine admiration for Westings. She declared that she could start her duties as soon as I wished and this was a relief to me. I felt that my equivocable position in the house would be easier once she was installed.

As the days went by I still felt pain at the thought that I was no longer the mistress of Westings, but I was getting used to the idea as one becomes accustomed to a physical affliction.

From Dr. Robbie, the Applebys and most of my friends I received a tactful sympathy. They implied, if they didn't actually say, that my father was more to be pitied than blamed.

"Thank God I'm not tempted now by a tight skin and a pretty pair of legs," said Dr. Robbie, frankly, when I went to Woodside for tea, soon after my return. He lowered his voice. "I'd sooner marry Mrs. Budge."

"Why don't you?" I said daringly, partly to hide my own emotion.

He shook his head with a faint smile and his gaze went to the portrait of his dead wife.

I saw nothing of Alan during my visit.

Poor Mary Peach showed some

embarrassment when I called upon her.

"Please believe me, Silla, I'd no idea Sir James was intending to marry again when I wrote to you," she said, with her tanned skin taking on a warmer glow. "Or I wouldn't have dreamed of intruding."

"Of course I believe it," I told her. "My father took us all by surprise."

There was a look in Mary's eyes that gave me a stab of remorse as she murmured: "As long as he's happy — "

How much I wished now that my father had married this old friend before ever Letta Price appeared on the scene.

As I had expected, Julia came back hot foot from Nice when she heard of her brother-in-law's mesalliance.

"Well, Jimmy, so you've turned to cradle-snatching in your old age," was her tart greeting to him.

"I can hardly claim to have reached old age yet, my dear Julia," was my father's calm reply, as he kissed her with his usual affection.

"You can say what you like about differences in age being of little account in marriage, but *forty years* difference between a husband and wife is a bit *too* much," declared Julia.

"Evidently Letta didn't think so," said my father, quite good temperedly.

Baffled, Julia turned the attack on Letta, when we three women were alone together in the best guest room.

"I hope you realise what you've taken on, my dear," she said, looking Letta up and down with a disdain that was only faintly concealed.

"But Jimmy is absolutely sweet," said Letta, opening her eyes wide and looking incredibly innocent.

"Hhm! May you long continue to think so!" said my aunt with a sniff, then added with superb effrontery: "I suppose you know all about the entail? I mean, you are aware that my brother-in-law can't leave Westings to anybody he likes?"

The insinuation couldn't be missed,

and I held my breath expecting fireworks from Letta. But she answered pleasantly.

"Oh yes," she said. "And I like your son, Julian, so much. I'm sure he'll make a wonderful owner for the dear old place. And isn't it marvellous that Silla is marrying him, and won't have to lose Westings, in spite of not being able to inherit it legally!"

Julia was completely taken-aback, which was quite something to see. But she rallied and answered: "Well, it will certainly be a very well matched affair, which is more than I can say for *some* marriages."

"Oh, do you think so?" said Letta, raising her eyebrows and speaking in a politely guarded tone.

I had a terrible desire to laugh.

"The impertinent little alley-cat!" exclaimed my aunt, when Letta had excused herself and drifted tactfully away. "Do you realise what she had the nerve to imply?"

"Yes," I said, looking her in the

eye but feeling myself blushing slightly. "She was hinting that I'm marrying Julian simply in order to be able to keep Westings."

"Utter nonsense!" said Julia warmly. "Why, you've been meant for each other from the cradle — *your* cradle I mean, of course. Darling, didn't I warn you against those Prices!"

"It was Adrian you warned me against," I pointed out.

"Well, brother and sister are evidently birds of a feather," said Julia. "Your father must have taken leave of his senses."

"Let's not talk about it any more, Julia," I pleaded.

"There's nothing we can do about it. We've just got to accept the situation."

"Is that what you've done?" she asked, looking at me with some scorn.

"It's what I'm trying to do," I said wearily, and she melted and embraced me tenderly,

Her visit was only a brief one, and Julian, too, never stayed more than a night or, at most a short week-end when he came. But life at Westings became livelier. News of my engagement and my father's new marriage attracted more visitors than usual. Some came out of curiosity, to see Letta, and I couldn't help admiring the way she rose to these occasions and showed a dignity and self-possession that were, I suppose, the result of her training as an actress.

She and my father and I began to work out a curious daily routine in which we kept out of one another's way as much as possible, so I really have no very clear idea how my young stepmother spent her time. Miss Russell proved to be a 'treasure' and took many of my past duties into her own capable hands. Adrian came and went between the lodge and London and was often at the house for luncheon or dinner, and I, for one, was always glad of his light-hearted company. Letta, too, seemed happier when he was present.

I can't say I never thought of Alan

Laird while the preparations for my wedding were going forward. He was like somebody shut in a cupboard at the back of my mind, whose knockings and cries to be let out I was determined to ignore.

And so we came to the day of the engagement party.

Because the wedding was to be so soon — some six weeks later — only a limited number of guests had been invited. These were relations and close friends and were mostly young people. A band had been hired and there was to be dancing.

Letta grew more and more animated as the time drew near. She had been up to London for a dress which she declared had 'cost the earth'. It was of white lace and looked distinctly bridal. I wondered if she wanted to compensate herself for the quiet wedding at the Registrar's Office. My own dress was a pale, sophisticated pink and Julian had given me a broach of pearls and sapphires to wear on it, and my father, on the morning of the party, clasped round my wrist a bracelet of pearls and sapphires which I knew he couldn't really afford.

"To be worn tonight for the first of many happy occasions, darling," he said, with a kiss. "There's an old belief that pearls mean tears, but these represent all my wishes for your happiness."

I thanked him with my arms round his neck and my cheek to his, but I had an awful feeling that he was giving and I was taking a bribe.

I remember old Benson and his assistant bringing in great armfuls of hot-house blooms, as well as humbler flowers from the garden. Peaches and big bunches of purple grapes were carried in also. Friedrich limped about giving orders to a band of helpers from the village, while Miss Russell gave contradictory instructions in his wake. Mrs. Dean and her own assistants toiled red-faced in the kitchen.

Adrian was very helpful, making

himself useful in all sorts of ways, shifting furniture, rolling up valuable rugs and giving his opinion as to where the flowers would best show to advantage. Later he drove Letta off to the hairdresser.

Lucille, Julia's Swiss maid, who was staying in the house with her employer, had promised to do my hair for me. She set it beautifully, in loose curls which she piled on top of my head and pinned. When I looked into the mirror I couldn't help feeling a lift in my spirits as I saw my reflection, regally coiffeured and bejewelled, staring back at me.

"You look very lovely, Silla," said my father, when I joined him in the hall downstairs. "Your mother would have been proud of you."

There was a wistfulness in his voice and eyes.

"And you look very handsome and distinguished, Daddy," I said, smiling. "And Letta is going to look quite ravishing in that new dress."

"She's as pleased as a child with it," he said, glancing at the Grandfather clock against the wall, which still kept excellent time, though it was over a hundred years old. "She should be ready by now."

Then she came, descending the stairs slowly, like the heroine of a musical, I thought rather unkindly. One expected her to throw out her arms and burst into song. But she gave a completely natural smile when she reached the bottom.

"Look, Jimmy. Like it?" she said eagerly, pirouetting in front of him.

"Charming, my dear," said my father indulgently.

She ran to him and kissed him lightly. "Thank you, darling. You've been so good to me," she sighed. Then she faced me. "Silla looks divine. And how marvellous the flowers are! Oh, I'm so excited!" And she danced a few steps.

To me there was something feverish about her gaiety. She seemed to be in the kind of mood a Scottish nurse I once had used to call fey. "I ken fine this will end in grief and woe," she would say. She was very often right.

The memory of that party has for me now all the glitter and unreality of a colourful charade. All the right things were said and done and the word the audience was supposed to arrive at was the little word 'Love'. But in the end the happenings of that night spelled out a very different word indeed.

Before the first guest arrived Julian and his mother joined us. Julia was in a beautifully cut black dress which showed off her white hair and her diamonds both to splendid advantage. Julian came to my side and gave my hand a quick squeeze.

"You look like the fairy come down from the Christmas Tree," he murmured.

"No. Letta looks like that," I whispered back rather ungratefully.

Then the party began with the arrival of an old school friend of mine, freckled and voluble. She was mad about horses, which was why, I decided, her escort looked exactly like a jockey.

It was a lovely evening. The weather combined summer warmth with the merest hint of autumn freshness. Doors and windows were left open so that guests could wander outside if they wished. Adrian had rigged up flood-lighting for the terrace and had hung softly tinted lights from the trees in the garden.

Having received everybody and made the usual sort of speech on these occasions, my father took himself off. Julia, too, drifted tactfully away after a while. I remember seeing Letta dancing with Adrian and with the jockey and once with Julian.

My fiancé and I danced together a good deal, of course, but there were times when we were separated for quite long periods. I talked and laughed and danced with everybody who asked me, but all the time I felt oddly detached, like a girl at somebody else's party.

In a little while it all seemed rather tiresome and silly, and I had a longing to get away. It was some time before the opportunity came, but at last, at a moment when everybody seemed to be engaged with somebody else, I picked up a stole and slipped out of the south door into the garden.

Adrian's lights were competing with the moon, which was shining softly down from a tranquil sky. I could see two shapes merging into one upon a garden seat not far away, so, not wishing to intrude, I went through the gate and round to the front of the house. The terrace was crowded with cars, but beyond I could see the lawn sweeping down to the lighter mass of the lake. I was warm and the air seemed deliciously sweet and cool.

The muted music of the band came to a pause, and in it I heard the quavering cry of an owl. It sounded like a comment. Then something darted across my feet and a small voice uttered an inviting chirrup. It was Angelique, in a gay and mischievous mood.

"Naughty puss!" I said, smiling. "What are you doing here?"

The little cat spent her nights in the kitchen, theoretically to scare away mice. She had a sanitary tray in the adjoining laundry-room, and was not supposed to be out at this dangerous hour, in case she made a dainty meal for a marauding fox.

Angelique waited now for me to come to her. Her tail was erect, her ears pricked. But just as I reached her, off she skipped and, delighted to make a fool of me, scampered down the broad stone steps that led from the gravelled terrace to the sloping lawn. Half-amused and half-annoyed at her antics, I followed.

My high heels sank into the soft turf, but I went on till I stood by the lake. There I looked about me, calling her name softly. But Angelique had vanished. I walked for a little way at the edge of the water, still calling. Then something whiter than the moonlight attracted my attention, some quite large object only a yard or so from the shore. I wondered if it could possibly be a sleeping swan. But as I approached it I saw that it was too large, and the wrong shape. A terrible idea came to me. The object really looked, I thought, like a half-submerged, half-floating body. It couldn't be, of course, it couldn't possibly be.

With appalled incredulity I leaned forward and peered down at the strange thing. Then I saw that it was Letta, in her belated bridal dress, her bright hair darkened with water, her sightless eyes staring up at the moonlight sky.

11

I KICKED off my shoes and waded into the water, forgetful of my delicate dress, till the cold water was up to my waist. There was a fur stole, like a drowned animal, lying in the water beside my stepmother. I struggled to lift her, to half-carry, half-drag her to the shore. She was small and light and I was tall and strong, but her sodden clothes made her heavy.

"Silla! My God! What are you doing?" Julian's startled voice rang out.

I looked round and saw him coming down the slope only a few yards away.

"Help me," I said simply. "I can't get her out."

He gave a kind of groan, then came splashing into the water. There was a smell of stagnancy and decay rising from the lake, where our feet had stirred up the silt. Between us, we got the limp wet shape onto the grass. Julian, who had not spoken again, turned Letta over on to her face and began trying to get the water out of her, while I stood and shivered.

"Go on," he shouted violently, turning his hand to glare up at me briefly. "Run to the house for help. Get brandy, blankets, hot water bottles. Phone for a doctor."

I ran as fast as I could up the grass slope, my cold wet dress clung to me, the gravel stung my feet painfully when I reached the terrace. All the time I knew that my haste was useless, that Letta was dead.

★ ★ ★

I burst into the hall, and the few people gathered there stared at me as if I had been the Westings ghost itself. I picked out too young cousins on my mother's side.

"There has been an accident, down by the lake," I gasped. "John, take some brandy down there and see if you can help. Sylvia, ask Miss Russell for blankets and hot water bottles."

Then I went to the phone and rang Woodside. It was Alan who answered, and his calm sane rather deliberate words were both a balm and a torment.

A couple of hours later I was sitting in the hall with my father, Julia, Julian and Adrian, sipping coffee which had been handed round by a yellow-faced Friedrich. Adrian had been weeping, and I wished that I could have wept too. I was full of pity and regret, but the tears wouldn't come.

The guests had all gone home, but the debris of the party remained. The breath of hot-house blooms, the fragrance of cigars and scented cigarettes mingled with expensive perfume and the fumes of alcohol, making a kind of background atmosphere. But in my nostrils still was the sickly, rotten smell of the stirred up lake, overcoming all the other civilized odours.

"I couldn't quite understand that Sergeant Whosit's attitude," said Julia suddenly.

She was still in her black dress and diamonds. It appeared that she and two middle-aged cousins of my father had been playing bridge upstairs in the study.

"Surely," continued my aunt, "the police don't suspect suicide."

We all stared at her.

"My dear, Julia, why should Letta have committed suicide?" asked my father, frowning.

"Why indeed?" said Julia. "That's what I'm saying."

"She didn't," I said. I was thinking of that fur stole in the water beside Letta. Nobody, I felt, would have drowned herself while clutching that round her.

"She was a very fortunate girl, I'm sure," declared my aunt. "She had no possible reason for taking her own life."

Adrian turned his handsome ravaged face towards her and gave her a look of pure hatred.

"You resented her," he said accusingly. He glared balefully round at the rest of us. "You all resented her. She was an intruder in your tight little privileged world. You hated her for that. And some of you were afraid, too."

"What nonsense!" said my aunt sharply.

Julian said nothing. He looked at his mother and glanced at me, then stared down at his hands.

"You're distraught, my boy," said my father gently to Adrian. "It's very understandable. I did my best for your poor sister, you know." He passed his slender hand over his face wearily.

"And much good it did her," said Adrian cruelly. He rose and stalked to the big main doors. "I shall be at the lodge if I'm wanted." He gave us a final look that seemed to reject us all utterly, before he went out.

"He's not responsible for what he

says, poor boy," said my aunt with conscious charity. "Jimmy, darling, you must go to bed. You look completely exhausted."

I saw that my father did indeed look frail and old and tired.

"Yes, do go to bed, Daddy," I said.

He gave us a wan smile and without a word, without pausing to give me his usual good night kiss, went slowly up the stairs, holding on to the banister rail as if for support.

"You should be in bed too, child," said Julia, turning her attention to me. "You've had quite a night."

"In a minute, Mother. I want to talk to Silla," said Julian.

"Don't keep her up too long then," ordered my aunt, rising. She kissed first her son and then me and climbed the stairs in her turn.

I wanted to go too, but the effort it would need to move from my chair seemed too great. I was wearing a warm housecoat, but every now and then I shivered.

"Silla." Julian spoke, leaning forward in his own chair and gazing at me intently. "How was it you came to be by the lake tonight? What were you doing there?"

I stared back at him. "I wanted a breath of fresh air, and you were nowhere near, so I just slipped out alone," I said. "Then I found Angelique on the terrace and meant to take her to the kitchen, but she ran away — in the direction of the lake, I followed her, and found what you know. Why were *you* there, Julian?"

I hadn't wondered about this before. Now I did.

"I was looking for you," he replied. "Sylvia said she thought she saw you going out into the garden. You didn't seem to be there, so I went round to the terrace. Then I saw somebody down by the lake and thought it looked like you."

He stared down at his hands again, "I suppose when I came along you were trying to pull Letta out," he added.

"Well, what did you think I was doing, pushing her down?" I said with tired irritability.

"No, of course not," he answered. His tone was very odd.

Incredibly, I realised that the conviction he had expressed was false. He was not at all certain that I had not been pushing Letta down.

I began to laugh. Once I had started I couldn't stop. I saw Julian's alarmed face and heard him entreating me to 'pull myself together and be sensible'. Then Julia came running downstairs, followed by her maid. She picked up a glass that had a little water in it and tossed the content lightly in my face.

I stopped laughing abruptly. "You shouldn't have done that, Julia," I said. "I've been wet enough once tonight." After that I wept quietly.

"Oh, *la pauvre petite*!" murmured Lucille. She took one arm and Julia took the other and between them they conducted me upstairs to bed as if I had been my Victorian great-great-aunt

236

in a fit of the vapours.

It was wonderful to lie in my own room in peace and quiet, though I couldn't stop shivering at first. Lucille brought me a hot drink and Julia insisted on my taking a couple of sleeping tablets with it and soon I began to feel drowsy.

Before I slept I had a picture of Alan's face in my mind, looking stern and still as he declared Letta to be beyond his skill. I wondered, with a sense of exhausted pain, if he too could be thinking I had pushed my young stepmother into the lake before making such efforts to pull her out. Then I slept like somebody who has been coshed into unconsciousness.

When I woke I heard a tapping at the door. It opened and Julia looked round it, paler than usual but with every silken hair in place.

"Oh, you are awake then," she said, entering. "I hope you feel better, my dear. But you mustn't think of getting up yet. Dr. Laird is downstairs. So are the police. Julian phoned for Dr. Robbie to come and say you weren't fit to be questioned this morning, but unfortunately that rude young man got the message and took it upon himself to come instead."

"I don't need a doctor," I said, sitting up. "And I'm perfectly able to be interviewed by the police or anybody else."

"Now, darling, don't go all haughty," said Julia, sitting on the side of the bed. "You're *not* well, you know. You were badly shocked last night. It was stupid of us not to have noticed earlier, but with all that gruesome business — "

She broke off, went to my dressing-table and peered critically into the mirror. "Poor Letta," she said, touching her exquisite coiffure. "Of course she must have been drunk when she fell in the lake."

"Did she drink all that much?" I said doubtfully. "I certainly shouldn't have thought so."

Julia stopped preening herself and her mirrored eyes met mine. "Then think so now," she said. "It's easily the best explanation for everyone's sake."

"Except Letta's," I murmured.

Julia walked to the door. "I'm bringing the doctor up in five minutes' time," she said, and went out.

When Alan came in I looked at his rather gaunt young face anxiously, for any sign of what he was thinking. But his expression was unreadable and his manner at first purely professional.

"You're not so bad," he pronounced, when he had felt my pulse and taken my temperature. "But there's no doubt you had a bad shock last night. Your — your relatives seem to think you're not well enough to be questioned by the police today. What do you yourself feel about it?"

We looked steadily at each other, and I thought again how bright and how blue his eyes were.

"Of course I'm well enough," I said. "I want to help all I can. But I did tell the police all I know last night."

"It was only a sergeant then. Now it's a superintendent," remarked Julia, with the faintest suggestion of a warning in her tone.

"A superintendent? I shall be glad to meet him," I said, and thought I saw a gleam of approval in Alan's eyes.

Suddenly I felt I must know if he shared the suspicion I felt sure was troubling Julian.

"My fiancé thinks I pushed my stepmother into the lake," I blurted.

"Drusilla!" cried Julia. "You can't know what you're saying. What will Dr. Laird think?"

"Dr. Laird thinks that Mr. Julian D'alquen must be a bad judge of character," said Alan, "and a poor sort of fiancé, too." And his eyes seemed almost to spark.

I felt a warm glow of happiness.

Then he marched to the door and turned, and he was stiff and unfriendly again.

"Young man you're impertinent," snapped Julia.

"I've taken a look at Sir James," said Alan, ignoring her. "He's bearing his loss with fortitude. Of course, he may not know the extent of it yet." He gave a wry sort of smile. "If I was superstitious I might think that curse you told me about was actually working." Then he went out.

"What on earth did he mean by that?" asked Julia.

"I don't know," I said. I was still quite rapturous within about Alan's championship of me. I threw back the bedclothes. "I'm going to get up," I told her.

"I think you're very unwise," declared Julia. "I hope Friedrich is showing that appalling young man out." And she sailed off to see.

But she sent up a breakfast tray, and I drank some orange juice and coffee and rejected most of the food. I thought about that parting remark of Alan's. Did he believe, as I sometimes did, that my father had married Letta in order to beget a son? Or had he meant something quite different? The loss not only of a wife but of a reputation, a privilege of privacy?

There were two men with my father in the study, when I entered. One was the youngish man I had seen the previous night, Sergeant Wells, and the other was an older, heavier man, with cool grey eyes, greying hair and a calm and authoritative manner.

My father greeted me gravely, and I thought again how old and tired he looked. He introduced the burly man as Superintendent Stone.

"Well, Miss D'alquen," said Mr. Stone, in a voice that had traces of a Midland accent, "I'm glad to see you're better. I hope you won't mind answering a few questions. Sir James says he would like to be present, so if you have no objection — "

"Of course not," I said. "But I'm afraid it may be very distressing for my father."

"It's distressing for us all, my dear," said my father quietly.

The superintendent went over my account of the finding of Letta's body in the lake, then he said: "I'm still not quite clear, Miss D'alquen, what took you down there, alone at that time of night, with a party going on in the house — and such a special party, too. To celebrate your engagement, wasn't it?"

"Yes. But I've explained," I said. "I badly wanted some fresh air. I happened for the moment to be alone, so — "

"Your fiancé, Mr. Julian D'alquen wasn't with you?" said Mr. Stone. He made this sound an odd thing.

"We couldn't be together the whole evening," I said rather impatiently. "We had a duty to the guests."

"Quite," said the superintendent significantly, as though he had made a point.

"I really don't see the point of your questions," said my father, leaning forward with a slight frown. "The accident to my wife can have nothing to do with — "

"Sir James," the superintendent interrupted, "I think I should tell you now that there is reason to believe Lady D'alquen was not drowned by accident."

"Not by accident?" said my father, sitting stiffly upright and staring at him strangely.

"She didn't commit suicide," I said. "She wouldn't. Besides — " I hesitated, while a feeling of horror began to creep over me.

"Yes," said Stone quickly.

"The stole. In that water," I said, and gulped.

He nodded, giving me a sharp look. Then he addressed my father again.

"We don't think Lady D'alquen committed suicide, either, Sir James," he said.

"But — but that leaves murder!" exclaimed my father incredulously.

"That's ridiculous!" I cried in a high

voice. But I knew there was something very wrong with my choice of words. "I can't believe it," I added.

But I could. In fact, at the back of my mind, pushed away and overlaid, the knowledge of murder had been lurking all the time.

"Couldn't she have been drinking and fallen in the lake when she was too drunk to get out," I suggested, not caring how brutal I sounded, so long as I didn't have to admit my intuitive knowledge.

"Did Lady D'alquen drink to excess?" asked Stone, raising his eyebrows.

"No, of course not," said my father sharply. "Drusilla, you don't know what you're saying."

I gave him a despairing glance.

"She had been drinking, yes," said the superintendent, nodding to me as if prepared in all reasonableness to go a little way with me. "But not enough to incapacitate her to the extent of allowing herself to drown in four feet of water. Somebody deliberately held her down under the water, Miss D'alquen, using her stole to bind her arms to her sides. There are marks to indicate this — marks that would probably have disappeared if her body had been left longer in the lake, as the murderer hoped, and indeed expected. Her long dress would have hampered her legs as she attempted to struggle." He spoke gravely, but quite calmly.

"But that's appalling!" I cried, feeling sick. "Who could possibly have done such a horrible thing?"

I had thought my father white-faced before. Now his pallor was quite corpse-like.

"Nobody at Westings," he said steadily. "It's unthinkable. Have you thought, Mr. Stone, that if your theory is right, the murderer would have got very wet himself. That surely would have betrayed him."

"Would it, sir?" said the superintendent quietly. His face was suddenly expressionless. "I believe Miss D'alquen was very wet when she came up to the house to get help. So was Mr. D'alquen. But that, of course, was due to their efforts in getting the poor lady *out* of the lake."

"Of course it was," I said loudly, feeling suddenly rather frightened of him.

"And you, Sir James, changed, I understand, in the course of the evening," the superintendent continued.

My father flushed slowly, holding the superintendent's eyes with his. "Only my jacket," he said. "I am always more comfortable in my old black velvet one."

"Mr. Price, too, had changed, and was at the lodge when he was told of his sister's death," said Mr. Stone. "He was intending to drive to London, where he was due on some film-set early this morning, he says."

"That's so," said my father. "I get your point, Mr. Stone. Among so many innocent reasons for changing it would be hard to find a guilty one."

"Exactly, sir," nodded the super-intendent. "Then there is a plastic mac and a pair of rubber boots in the little boat-house where the dinghy is kept. They were damp and muddy when found, but Mr. Price says he put them on to get at some bulrushes just before the party. He wanted to add them to the flower arrangements."

"Yes," I said. "That's quite true. But you mean that somebody else could have put them on later, and it wouldn't show."

"But think of the risk," cried my father. "If they had been seen — "

"There would have been a risk. Yes," said Mr. Stone. "But not a very great one, Sir James. Your guests were mostly young people, keeping in couples when they went outside and not likely to stray far from the house. The ladies were wearing high narrow heels, too, unsuitable for walking on the soft ground. The place where the body was found is not easily seen until you get right down beside the lake."

"But who *would* have done such a thing, even if they could have done it without much danger of detection?" said my father in a troubled voice.

"Somebody who desperately wanted Lady D'alquen out of the way," replied the superintendent promptly, with a hardening of look and voice. He turned to me. "Your stepmother wasn't much older than you, Miss D'alquen. Did she confide in you at all?"

"Confide in me?" I repeated, feeling guilty. "In what way?"

"She didn't tell you, by any chance, that she was in the early stages of pregnancy?" he asked.

12

MY father made an inarticulate sound, and the superintendent turned his cold gaze upon him. "*You* didn't know either, sir?" he said. "Well, ladies do generally keep their own council till they are certain in these matters. But there's no doubt about it. About four weeks, the doctors say."

My father said nothing. His face wore a curiously still and inward looking expression.

"I'm very sorry, Sir James," said the superintendent, and the sergeant murmured an agreement. "If the child had been born and had been a boy he would have inherited Westings and the baronetcy, I suppose."

"Yes," said my father slowly and heavily, "he would have inherited Westings and the baronetcy."

I felt a great wave of pity for him and for Letta. I wanted to weep for the cruel and tragic waste, and suddenly I was deeply ashamed of my own selfish fear of the birth of a son to my father and his new young wife. Then I thought of Alan's words about the curse still working, and now I knew what he had meant.

"Oh Daddy, I'm so sorry," I exclaimed.

His eyes still had that blind look, but he murmured: "Thank you. Thank you."

The superintendent rose. So did the quietly observant sergeant. Both men looked at my father with a kind of curiosity, strongly mixed with sympathy in Sergeant Well's case.

"Thank you for being so helpful," said the superintendent formally.

My father became aware that they were taking their leave and rose to his feet.

"Ring for Friedrich to show these gentlemen out, darling," he murmured.

251

"Good morning, Mr. Stone, Sergeant."

The superintendent paused in the doorway. "Of course, we aren't forgetting the possibility that whoever killed the poor lady was somebody who knew her when she was an actress," he said. "Some jilted — that is some man who fancied himself ill used when she married you, sir. It would have been easy for him to get into the grounds."

"Yes," said my father, without at all pressing the point, "quite easy."

When we were alone he sat down again and stared silently at nothing. I had a longing to reach him, to let him know of my remorseful sympathy.

"Daddy," I said, going close to him. "If you and poor Letta had had a baby son, I expect I would have loved him myself. After all, he would have been my brother, and I always wanted some siblings."

He looked at me then, and his expression changed.

"My darling girl," he said. "You don't think the child Letta was going to have was mine, do you? It couldn't possibly have been. Not possibly. Our marriage — Well, let us call it a marriage of companionship only."

I stared at him blankly, and he took my hand and spoke very gently:

"I know it has been very hard for you to understand," he said, "but everything I have done has been for your sake. Since you were a very little girl you have come first with me."

He rose and kissed me tenderly then walked to the door. "You and Westings," he said, and went out.

I stood feeling quite stunned by this new revelation. Letta pregnant by some unknown man. My father's marriage little more than a formality. But why, why, why? And what had he meant by saying that everything he had done had been for *my* sake? *What* had he done?"

And then a terrible fear came to me. Suppose it was my father himself who had held Letta under the cold malodorous water of the lake till she was dead. I clasped my head and told myself I must be going mad. It wasn't true. Of course he could never have done such a thing. Not my kind, gentle, high-principled father. It was as fantastic to suspect him as for Julian to suspect me, or for my father to suspect Julian.

The last thought came to me casually then stayed. After all, it was Julian who would have lost the most by the birth of a son to Letta. How much would he have minded? I remembered the sudden way my cousin had appeared at the lakeside at the appropriate moment the previous night, and asked myself if his clothes could possibly have been wet *before* he had entered the water to help me with my rescue attempt.

Then the door opened and Julia appeared. "Oh, there you are, darling" she said. "Don't stay up here moping. Luncheon is nearly ready. It was past twelve when you came downstairs, you know."

"I can't eat anything," I said.

"Nonsense! Of course you must eat," said my aunt. "Starving yourself won't bring that poor girl back. It will only add to poor Jimmy's worries."

There was truth in this and I went with her meekly, prepared to try to carry on as usual. Julian was in the hall with my father. Through the long windows I could see men moving about beside the lake. Angelique, who had led me to my terrible discovery, now lay curled innocently on the cushion of one of the deep chairs.

Julian came to meet me and kissed me. "I'm afraid we were neither of us quite ourselves last night," he said softly. "After such a terrible business it's not surprising. The future's going to be rather grim, too. Westings is in for some unpleasant publicity. I'll be here as much as I can be and Mother is going to stay. Thank God Beresford is coming down."

Mr. Beresford was the family solicitor; still is, for that matter.

It seemed to me that I suddenly

became sane. Of course Julian had not killed Letta. It was unthinkable. Unthinkable, too, that my father had committed such a crime. It must have been, as Superintendent Stone had suggested, a man from my stepmother's past.

I relaxed and became at ease again with Julian. But I wondered if he knew of Letta's pregnancy. It was not the sort of fact my father would be anxious to discuss with anybody. On the other hand news of it was bound to come out.

I thought about it while we four sat at lunch, all rather silent and abstracted. If the pregnancy was of about a month's duration, then it had begun at the time of her marriage to my father. Who could have been responsible for it? Some man in her own profession, whom she had been meeting in London? Or a local lover?

Then I remembered what Adrian had said when he had discussed his sister's marriage with me. Not that I had ever forgotten. But now it had a new significance. He had actually been afraid that Letta would become a doctor's wife, he had said, because she had been so fascinated by 'our craggy Dr. Kildare'. Alan! The man he had described as being of 'the puritan type' with 'hints of banked up fires and volcanoes of passion liable to break out at any minute'.

I felt sick suddenly and put dawn my knife and fork abruptly and rose.

"I'm sorry," I said. "I — I think I'll go and lie dawn."

"Darling! You do look rough," exclaimed Julian.

"I'll ring for Friedrich to take you up some brandy," said my father. "Perhaps you ought to see the doctor again."

"Dr. Robertson this time, and not that young Laird," said Julian, with a frown.

"Don't be silly, dear," said Julia, to my surprise.

"Dr. Laird has impossible manners,

but he's much more efficient than dear old Robbie."

"Then why is he burying himself down here?" Julian demanded to know, rather aggressively.

"I'm sure I don't know," replied his mother. "Perhaps he drinks or chases women. It seems most unlikely, but nothing will surprise me any more. Would you like me to come up with you, Silla, darling?"

I refused her offer, and went up to my room alone. I felt a little better after the brandy, but I longed to see Alan again. I thought that if I could look into his eyes I would know whether there was any truth in this latest suspicion of mine. But I was ashamed to either send for him or go to see him.

I couldn't of course, go on playing the invalid and skulking in my room, so after a while I went downstairs again. On my way I passed the door of my father's study and was interested to hear Mr. Beresford's voice coming from within. I had known 'young Beresford', as my father called him, since my earliest childhood and he had always seemed to me quite middle-aged, but his father had then only recently retired from the firm and he was certainly young compared with 'old Beresford'. He is a large man with a fine ringing voice who would have made a good barrister.

I paused a moment, wondering whether to go in and greet him. It was then I heard him cry: "Confess to the police? Not if I can help it, Sir James!"

I stood still, with all my nightmare fears rushing back, not even considering that I was eavesdropping. My father spoke, but I couldn't hear what he said. Then the solicitor chipped in, his voice quieter now. I caught only one word. It was 'madness'. After that there was more conversation, till Mr. Beresford's voice rang out loudly again. "But is this young doctor to be trusted?" he cried.

Then realisation of what I was doing sent me hurrying on towards the stairs.

But already a terrifying explanation of the few words I had overheard was going through my mind.

What could it be that Mr. Beresford would not let my father confess to the police but that he had himself killed Letta? And that word 'madness'. If my father had really crowned his wife then it must have been while temporarily insane. Perhaps he had cared for her more than it seemed. Perhaps the non-consummation of the marriage had been her doing and not his, and she had told him of her pregnancy, taunted him with the idea that her child by some stranger would be legally a D'alquen and might one day inherit Westings. Such provocation might well turn the brain of a proud and sensitive man. Wasn't that impulsive and unsuitable marriage itself evidence that my father had not been his normal self for some time?

I didn't want to believe any of this. There was a part of my mind that refused to believe it. But my reason told me that it was an explanation that accounted for a good deal. There was the reference to Alan, too. I had decided that the 'young doctor' mentioned by Mr. Beresford could only refer to him. Miserably I wondered if my father, too, suspected that he might be the man responsible for Letta's condition. He might even know it, though he had certainly seemed surprised when Mr. Stone had told us of the pregnancy. People who were mentally sick could be cunning, though.

I tortured myself with similar doubts and suspicions till the day of the inquest. It was well attended, by local busybodies as well as by the press. The coroner was a small elderly man named Barnes. I was aware of furtive stares and whispers as my father and I took our places in the seats reserved for us. Adrian, who looked handsomer than ever, in a haggard way, was already close by and he shifted his chair a little and wouldn't meet my eye after one glance towards us.

Then I realised that Alan was present, with Dr. Robbie beside him. And when I saw those clear, shatteringly honest blue eyes looking at me, my heart lifted and I knew that never in a thousand years would the owner of them have played the part Letta's lover had done. I came to my senses in that respect at least.

We had been told that the proceedings were to be merely a formality, but Mr. Beresford had thought it advisable to be present.

Adrian gave evidence of identity, which he did with what the newspapers next day called 'visible emotion', and I felt very sorry for him. Then I myself was called upon to say how I had discovered Letta in the lake. When the police surgeon declared that she had met her death by drowning he made no mention of her pregnancy.

We all thought it was the end of that particular hearing when the coroner granted the request for an adjournment made by Superintendent Stone. But

Adrian suddenly got to his feet again.

"Mr. Stone," he cried in his carrying actor's voice.

"I want to make it public now that my sister was murdered. And I know *why* she was murdered. She was pregnant, and her condition was too great a threat to too many people."

Instantly Mr. Beresford was on his feet also.

"Mr. Coroner, I object on behalf of my distinguished and bereaved client to the uncalled for remarks made by Mr. Price," he declared, in tones that matched Adrian's. "Allowance must be made, of course, for his state of shock and grief, but my client has also been subject to similar stresses. I hope you will not permit any further demonstrations, sir."

"Certainly not," the coroner assured him, slightly flushed and very firm of voice. "Mr. Price, we all sympathise with you, but we really cannot allow you to make wild accusations here. The inquest is adjourned." And he rose and fairly scampered out.

My father had kept perfectly quiet and still, staring straight in front of him. In silence, with a hand on my arm, he walked out, while Mr. Beresford fended off reporters and others who approached us, like a well-trained guard dog.

Outside, he allowed Dr. Robertson to come up to us, however.

"A bad business, James, a bad business!" said Dr. Robbie with a sigh, as he shook hands with my father.

"Dr. Robertson," said Mr. Beresford quickly, in a low voice, as the old doctor greeted me affectionately. "I wonder if you and Dr. Laird would be good enough to come back with us to Westings Court. Sir James wishes to consult you both on a very important matter."

Dr. Robbie looked surprised.

"Please, Robbie," murmured my father.

"Well, we mustn't stay long and we'll have to leave word where we can be found," said the old doctor. "I'll speak to Alan and if he's willing we'll follow you."

We got into the Humber and were driven home by Friedrich. Looking back once, I saw Alan's car not far behind, with Dr. Robbie's saloon sedately bringing up the rear. It struck me that it was almost like a funeral procession, a rehearsal for the next day's sad ceremony.

When we arrived at Westings the four men went upstairs to the study and were closeted there for some time. A call came asking for one of the doctors to go to a neighbouring farm where a man had injured himself by a fail from a loft. But it was Robbie who went and Alan who remained another twenty minutes with my father.

I thought I knew what was going on. I had read somewhere that two medical men must examine a patient before he could be certified insane. My father believed that he was going to be charged with Letta's murder and was intending to plead insanity. It was a sign of the unhappiness and confusion of mind that afflicted me then that this idea actually gave me hope.

There were no relatives of the dead woman at her funeral, except Adrian. The time of the ceremony had been kept secret so that it could be as private as possible. Adrian maintained his hostile attitude to my father and to me, even by the graveside. My father responded with patience and a lack of resentment that would have seemed admirable if it had not been for those dark suspicions of mine.

We drove back to Westings in a sunshine that seemed to mock the occasion. Adrian had curtly refused a lift.

"Poor child!" said my father suddenly. "She had a natural gaiety. She deserved something better than this."

The remark came just as I was remembering Letta at Nanny's funeral, and how amusing she had been afterwards. It seemed hard to realise that it had been only two months ago.

When we got back to the house Friedrich handed my father an envelope.

"Mr. Price left it, just after you had gone to the funeral, sir," he said. "I hope it did not make him late."

"No, Friedrich. He wasn't late," said my father.

I thought his hand trembled slightly as he took the envelope from the salver, and opened it. Something fell with a tinkle. It was a key. Friedrich picked it up, gave it to my father and softly went away.

"An unfriendly little note saying that he is giving up the lodge and going back to London permanently," said my father, looking up from the letter.

"It's just as well, Jimmy," said Julia, and went upstairs to put away her mink and her elegant black suit and most becoming hat. The card attached to her wreath — orchids again — had been suitably inscribed from herself and Julian.

"Daddy," I said quietly, as he slowly and thoughtfully tore up the letter. "*Is* Adrian related to us?"

He gave me a strange look. "He's my brother-in-law, if that's what you mean," he said.

"You know it isn't," I said bluntly. "I mean was his father and Letta's really the son of Great Uncle Charles?"

He merely shrugged and turned away. "It can't matter one way or the other now, my dear," he said.

I suppose that he was right, but there the question was, with the other more terrible ones, to trouble me.

It was three days later that I had a very surprising phone call. Friedrich had told me that a gentleman who would not give his name wished to speak to me and I picked up the receiver half-expecting it to be the representative off some newspaper, though so far we had been very little troubled in this way. I was agreeably disappointed.

"Listen, Silla," said Alan Laird's voice, speaking quietly but urgently.

"I've something very important and very private to tell you. Something that concerns your father as well as yourself. The lodge is empty now, I believe. Can you meet me there this evening, at about nine?"

"Yes," I said simply.

"Good. Don't tell anybody about this. I'll explain when we meet," said Alan softly.

When I replaced the receiver I found that my breath was coming fast. I thought I knew what Alan had to say to me. He meant to warn me of what was pending, a charge against my father and a defence of temporary insanity. But, in a sense, I was going to an assignation and that sweetened the bitterness for me.

About half an hour after receiving the call I suddenly remembered that Julian was coming down that evening. It might be difficult for me to slip away unnoticed.

I rang Woodside, but Mrs. Budge told me that both doctors were out.

Of course she asked if I would leave a message and I said that there was no need and it was all quite unimportant.

Then I wrote a little note, explaining, and asking Alan to wait if I should not be at the lodge by nine or soon after. I remember I tied a headscarf over my hair and put on dark glasses to walk to the village, for there was always the danger now of being accosted by reporters, or even photographed. But I reached the doctor's house without being stopped and managed to slip the note through the letter-box unobtrusively and hurry away.

As it happened, I need not have worried about the difficulties of getting away from Julian. Immediately after dinner my father, who had been very silent throughout the meal, turned to my cousin, and spoke.

"I wonder if you would mind coming up to my study, Julian. I want to talk to you. If Silla has no objection, of course."

I said I hadn't, and Julian went

upstairs with him. Was everybody to be taken into his confidence except myself? I wondered with some pain. But Julia was obviously also in the dark.

"Something to do with the estate, I suppose," she said, and yawned gracefully. "I hope they won't stay talking too long. I had hoped for a game of Bridge. One must pass the time somehow and television is so boring."

I murmured something about taking the dogs for a walk, and escaped. It was just nine o'clock, and already dark. The great cedar made a huge black shape against the dim sky and the avenue was a tunnel of mysterious gloom. But these were familiar things and I was not nervous because of them, as I walked quietly along, but only because I felt the meeting I was to have with Alan must be a momentous one.

There was no sign of him when I reached the lodge. Glad that I had arrived first, I let myself in, leaving the front door ajar, and went into the little sitting-room, switching on the light and drawing the pretty curtains poor Letta had made. I had no wish to be seen there with Alan by anybody passing along the road about a hundred yards away.

Then I thought suddenly how Letta had wanted window-boxes, and I looked round me with a feeling of regret and sadness. Adrian had taken little away, for most of the furniture had come from the house. It all looked much the same as when the gay young couple had first set up housekeeping here. I thought how little any of us could have foreseen then either Letta's amazing marriage or her tragic death.

I heard a step outside in the box of a hall and turned ready to face Alan, feeling a thrill of pleasure and excitement mingling with my dread of what I felt sure he would tell me.

But it was not Alan who stood in the doorway staring at me. It was Adrian. He was wearing a raincoat with the collar turned up and a hat with the brim turned down. I had never seen him in a hat before. Then I saw that he had shaved off his little beard, and when he tilted the hat back and smiled at me he looked like the old light-hearted Adrian. "Hullo Silla," he said pleasantly. "Beautiful as ever, I see!"

"Hullo," I said, relieved at the restoration of his easy friendly manner. "I thought you were in London."

"I've come back for something," he said, and he stopped smiling and looked at me with a curious intentness. "Do you want to know what it is?"

"Not particularly," I answered in surprise. "I mean, it's not my business."

"I think you ought to know, all the same," he told me, still with that strange look. "Go to that bureau behind you and open the right-hand drawer. You'll find a letter inside."

He seemed so much in earnest that I turned and did as he said. Lying in the drawer was a photograph of Letta — a studio portrait — smiling and pretty. On it was a piece of folded paper. I took it out and turned round again.

"Is this it?" I asked as I did so.

Then I started and dropped the letter. I stared incredulously, for Adrian was holding a revolver pointed straight at my heart, and his eyes were full of deadly purpose.

13

INSTINCTIVELY I tried to pretend he was fooling.

"Oh dear!" I said, with a smile that must have been just a stiff grimace. "Are you trying to frighten me?"

"Yes," he said harshly. "And I'm succeeding, aren't I?"

"Adrian! Don't be silly. What have *I* done to you?" I said. I still couldn't really believe he was serious, in spite of the expression in his eyes.

"You killed Letta," he answered, keeping that menacing little barrel steadily pointing.

"But I didn't," I gasped. "Adrian, I swear to you that I didn't."

"Then it was your father," he said grimly.

"No!" I cried.

"No? Perhaps you're right," he said, and suddenly his voice and his eyes were mocking me. "You and that bright young executive, Cousin Julian, had the best motive. And you're tall and strong, aren't you, Silla, in spite of that slender figure."

He gave a laugh that was far from pleasant to hear.

"How condescending you were to the common young Prices," he sneered. "Until you saw the danger of losing all your chances of being the Lady of Westings for the rest of your comfortable life."

I was frightened and bewildered but I said as quietly and sincerely as I could: "I certainly never thought of Letta or you as 'common young Prices' and I'm sorry if you thought I did. Now will you please be sensible and put away that gun?"

He smiled again but his eyes were hard and watchful. "It's your father's gun," he said. "I borrowed it — without asking of course — when I was up at the house, visiting my distinguished brother-in-law. But it won't have my fingerprints on it when it's found. It will have yours."

I began to believe then that he really meant to kill me. But he couldn't. I was too young. I hadn't achieved anything, not even happiness. I thought of Alan with longing. Alan! He was coming here to meet me! Adrian couldn't know that. Hope sprang alive in me.

"You can't shoot me now," I cried. "You'll be caught. Dr. Laird is due here any minute."

I had been aware of cars passing along the motor-road from time to time. How I strained my ears to hear one approaching. There had been two together a little while before, and now it occurred to me that one of them might have stopped. Then I saw that Adrian was grinning at me with an evil amusement.

"So Dr. Laird is due, is he?" he said. Voice and expression changed again. "Listen, Silla, I've something very important and very private to tell you. Something that concerns your father as well as yourself."

It might have been Alan himself speaking.

"That phone call! *You* made it," I said, and felt hope give way to despair.

"Of course. There's some advantage in being a professional actor, and a good one too," he said boastfully.

I could sense a growing and terrifying excitement in him.

"Now say your prayers," he told me, "and a bit more fervently than you've ever done in the D'alquen pew in dear Mr. Appleby's church."

I didn't pray. I didn't have time. Because suddenly there was a miracle. Alan was there, standing in the doorway right behind Adrian, his face tense and pale and his brilliant eyes seeming to flash a message at me.

Then with startling swiftness he acted. Almost simultaneously Adrian's arm was jerked up, there was an explosion, a bit of plaster fell from the ceiling and the revolver clattered to the floor.

Alan flung Adrian aside, pounced on the weapon and came upright again in a moment.

"Now, Price, go and stand against that wall," he said. He was breathing a bit hard, but his voice was steady. "And don't give me a chance to shoot you." His blue eyes shone menacingly. "Because I'd like fine to do it. You'd not appreciate a bullet in your leg where I'd put it."

Adrian had looked frightened and furious, but he had recovered quickly. He did as he was told, but he did it as if he were indulging Alan in some ridiculous dramatics.

"I thought it was a doctor's job to mend bones, not break them," he said. "You're very violent for a respectable medical man." He gave a laugh that almost convinced. "You don't really think I was going to shoot poor little Silla, do you?"

"I do," said Alan. Then with a different note in his voice, he asked, without looking away from Adrian:

"Are you feeling all right, Silla? Sit down and put your head between your knees, if not."

I fought a hysterical desire to laugh. "Yes, I'm all right," I said, and added shakily: "I think."

"I was only trying to scare her into confessing that she had killed Letta," said Adrian, but while he spoke he kept glancing towards my feet.

I looked down and saw the folded paper I had taken from the drawer and had dropped. I stooped to pick it up, and Adrian made a slight jerky movement, then looked warily at Alan and stayed still.

I unfolded the paper and was staring in horror at the words written on it, when I heard Rollo's bark outside and a quick command from Julian. Then my cousin appeared in the doorway, blinking and amazed.

"What's going on?" he said. "Good God! Are you mad, Laird? And Silla! Mother said you had taken the dogs for a walk, but I found them in the hall."

"Price was about to murder her when I came," said Alan curtly.

"It's true, Julian," I gasped. But I was looking at Adrian and he was gazing at me. I with an increasing horror of realisation and he with an indescribable mixture of chagrin and mockery and pride.

"Why you horrible little swine!" cried Julian. "I'll get the police. Or had Silla better go? The lodge isn't on the phone. You might need my help, Laird."

"The police are here, I think," said Alan. "I phoned them before I came, when I got home and found Silla's note and realised something was wrong here."

I had heard, too, the car stop and doors slam. Then there were quick footsteps and barking dogs and suddenly the little room seemed full of people, though there were only two newcomers, Sergeant Wells and a uniformed policeman.

"I'm glad you've come, Sergeant,"

said Alan. "I'm charging this man, Adrian Price, with enticing Miss D'alquen to this place with intent to murder her."

"It's all nonsense," said Adrian. He tried to speak lightly, but he was pale now and his eyes watched me holding the paper. "It was just a harmless trick."

"A trick, yes. But harmless, no," I said bitterly. "This note. Do you know what it says?"

I looked round at them all then read aloud in a voice I could hear tremble: "I'm sorry, I'm sorry. Poor Letta. I don't know what devil possessed me to do that to her. I am taking the best way out for all. Perhaps when I am dead I shall be forgiven. It's signed with my name and it's in my writing. But I didn't write it. I didn't write it."

Julian had his arm round me. "Darling!" he murmured. "Oh darling!"

"Of course you didn't," said Alan, matter of factly, still keeping his gaze

on Adrian, and the revolver ste.
pointing. "Price is a forger on
of everything else. But I've a pie.
of news for him. Are you listening,
Price? Maggie McLean couldn't read
or write till she was nearly forty. Her
son taught her. *I* found that out for
Sir James. I come from Glenairlie,
you see."

This statement seemed so utterly
irrelevant that I stared at him as if
he had gone out of his mind.

"What does that matter?" I cried.
"Don't you understand? He was going
to kill me and make me take the blame
for Letta's murder. People would have
thought I'd committed suicide."

"Yes, yes," said Julian, tightening
his hold of me, then turning to the
sergeant asked fiercely: "What are you
going to do about it, Wells?"

"We are taking Mr. Price to the
station for questioning, sir," replied
Sergeant Wells. "We intended to do
that in any case, when we knew he
was back."

and suppose I won't come," said
rian.

"You will," said Alan grimly.

"I don't think you'll need that
revolver any more, sir," said the
sergeant tactfully, with a large palm
extended. "Perhaps you'll come with
us too, doctor. I can see the young
lady has had a shock. If Mr. D'alquen
likes to take her back to the house we
can get her statement later."

Alan looked at me then, but very
briefly, and his glance went immediately
to Julian at my side. "Yes, take her
home, D'alquen," he said.

Then he gave up the revolver and, as
the police officers closed in on Adrian,
turned away.

Adrian gave a shrug, as if humouring
the company, and walked to the door
with his escort. But he was still very
pale and there was a look of strain now
about his mouth and eyes.

At the door he seemed to rally a little.
He turned and looked back. "Good-
bye, Cousin Silla, Cousin Julian,"

he said with a twisted little smile. "It's been nice knowing my grand relations."

The two policemen looked rather strangely at us, and Julian and I glanced at each other. We said nothing.

As we walked back to the house I was glad of the comfort of his arm round me. We hardly spoke at all.

Later I made up for my silence by being very voluble, wanting to tell my story over and over again, to my pale and anxious father and an astonished Julia, to Superintendent Stone and to Dr. Robbie, whom Julian had sent for.

"Alan saved my life," I told the old doctor, finally. "Do you realise that? He saved my life and I never even thanked him."

"He'll understand. Alan's a good lad," said Dr. Robbie, most inadequately, I felt.

I was more satisfied when my father said: "I owe that young man more and more, it seems, and this last debt I never can repay."

Then I was ordered off to bed and given two sleeping-pills.

I woke late next morning and was brought breakfast in bed. I had hardly finished it when there was a tap on the door, and Julian entered.

He seemed subdued and greeted me rather gravely, making no comment when I turned my head as he stooped to kiss me so that his lips touched my cheek and not my mouth.

"I thought we ought to talk, Silla," he said, sitting on the side of the bed. "So, if you're well enough — "

"There's nothing wrong with me," I said impatiently, "and I'm not going to be treated like an invalid and have things kept from me."

"Good," he said, with a nod. "Well, Stone has been here this morning and has told us a good deal. Adrian Price has been charged with the murder of Letta."

"But I don't understand," I cried. "Why should he have killed his own sister?"

"She wasn't his sister. She was his mistress," said Julian.

"Good heavens!" I stared at him, while he poured out more information.

"Apparently the real Violet Price went to Australia some years ago and married out there. Letta's real name was Fay Goodman. I think she and Adrian pretended to be brother and sister in the first place because — well both of them relied a good deal on their sexual attractions for their advantages and advancements and any known attachments would have cramped their style."

"Then he killed her out of jealousy," I guessed.

Julian shook his head. "No. It was *his* idea she should marry your father."

"Adrian's idea?" I was more puzzled than ever.

"Uncle James took me into his confidence, yesterday, Silla," said Julian, "and he has asked me now to pass on to you what he told me, to spare him having to confess to you direct."

"Yes?" I said, half-fearful of what might be coming, though if Adrian had murdered my stepmother then my past dreadful suspicions must have been far from the truth.

"After you and Mother had gone to Nice, Adrian told your father that he had made a discovery," said Julian. "He said that before Nanny had died she had hinted that he and Letta were really descended from Charles D'alquen and not from her husband, William Price. Naturally he had assumed that the old lady had meant illegitimately descended."

"Of course," I said, opening my eyes wide.

"Well, he had found, he said, a letter among her papers from a woman called Maggie McLean," Julian continued.

"Oh!" I exclaimed, remembering Alan's mysterious announcement.

"You know our great-grandfather once had a house in Scotland, where all the family used to go for August and September, when my father and Uncle

James were little boys?" said Julian.

"Yes. It was at Glenairlie — where Alan comes from," I said.

"So it seems." He gave me a quick look. "Well, Nanny used to be one of the party and apparently she made friends with this Maggie McLean, who was a crofter's daughter. They kept up the friendship — or rather picked it up later, I think — and Nanny had letters from her right up to the time of the woman's death some twelve years ago. But this particular letter was written — or supposed to have been written — fifty-seven years ago. It said that Maggie was quite excited to know that Nanny was to have a bairn, and what a fine inheritance it would have, if it was a boy. She would keep her promise not to breathe a word about the secret marriage to Mr. Charles D'alquen till Nanny said she could."

"Secret marriage!" I exclaimed.

"Yes. You can see the implications," said Julian grimly. "Great Uncle Charles was the elder son. If Adrian's father

289

was his legitimate son — "

"Then Westings and the baronetcy belong by rights to Adrian and not to my father," I finished. "Oh poor Daddy!"

"Yes, but he said he was more greatly concerned for us — for you in particular," Julian said. "And I believe him," he added quietly and sincerely.

"Oh so do I," I said. Then I begged him to go on.

"Uncle James says the letter looked genuine. The paper seemed old and the ink faded, the writing appeared to be much the same as in the later letters Nanny had received from Maggie. Of course he said he would hand the matter over to Beresford without delay. But he admits that he was scared. Adrian said that he knew what the D'alquen solicitors would say, that possession was nine points of the law and that if it had been a Scottish marriage there might be no record of it and, having taken place so long ago, no witnesses living."

I interrupted again. "That's true. But Daddy has a conscience."

"Adrian counted on that," said Julian. "But he said that he would also put the matter into the hands of a solicitor, but it would be rather a grim joke if the case went to court and cost so much that the estate wouldn't be worth having in the end. That worried Uncle James more than ever and he was just about ripe for Adrian's suggested solution."

"Which was that Daddy should marry Adrian's supposed sister and both should cry quits," I cried, understanding suddenly not only the strange marriage but my father's attitude to it, and why he had said that he had acted throughout mainly for my sake.

Julian nodded. "Ingenious, wasn't it?"

"And the child Letta was going to have was really Adrian's?"

"Yes. I'm sure that was part of the plan. Once a son had been born Uncle

James would have been quietly done away with."

"Oh no!" I cried, horrified.

"Oh yes," said Julian grimly. "It makes sense — Adrian's kind of sense. He would have been sitting pretty for the rest of his life, milking Letta, who would never have dared to cast him off. Your father thinks she had already given him money, settled some bills of his and bought him that horse."

"But suppose somebody had recognised her as Fay Goodman," I said.

"I don't think it would have mattered much," said Julian. "Letta was an actress and people could have thought that either the Letta Price or the Fay Goodman was merely a stage name."

"What went wrong with the plan? Why did Adrian kill her?" I asked.

"Two things went wrong," Julian said. "First, your father wouldn't co-operate properly. Secondly, Letta lost her nerve. Remember that nightmare? And she *had* been drinking more than usual on the night of the party, you know. I think Adrian saw that he could no longer rely on her, and I'm pretty sure she knew more against him than that he was guilty of forgery and conspiracy. I think she knew that he had been guilty of murder too."

"Murder! What murder?" I asked.

"Nanny's," said Julian. "Think how conveniently the poor old lady died. If she had lived there could have been no such plot carried out. She would have known the letter was a forgery and she would have denied the marriage."

"Yes," I said, beginning to be wise after the event. "In any case I don't see how Daddy could really have believed that Nanny would have kept silent about that."

"Adrian made it seem very possible," said Julian. "He pointed out that Nanny had been a simple country girl and that she had had a great awe and respect for the D'alquen family. She had been first deserted by Charles and then widowed and had married William Price on impulse and in a panic. Afterwards she had become too devoted to us all to want to see us disinherited by any act of hers."

"Yes, it does sound plausible," I agreed. "And you think Adrian murdered his own grandmother so that she couldn't deny all this. How horrible! But how could he have done it? He wasn't there that day. Don't you remember? He and Letta went to London."

"A poisoner doesn't have to be present at the death of his victim," said Julian. "And there were Nanny's own concoctions all handy. He simply had to increase the concentration of the digitalis."

I shivered, thinking of that day in Nanny's bedroom, when I had looked out of the window at the great cedar and seen — what I had seen? Some shadow of evil cast by that couple in the room? Some recent wrong taking the form of an old one? Or simply the Westings ghost evoked by the threat to Westings heirs? Wiser ones than I will have to decide. But I understood better Letta's terror and Adrian's white face. For a moment they had looked at their own guilt.

"After Adrian had killed Letta he was afraid that it would be only a matter of time before they found her true identity and suspected him, unless he could provide a scapegoat," went on Julian. "That's why he started pointing the finger at us, and why finally he decided to plant the guilt on you and fake your suicide."

"And if it hadn't been for Alan — " I said, and began to glow. "He really proved that the letter was a forgery," I added quickly.

"Yes. It was a bit of luck, Laird having come from Glenairlie and having a grandfather still living in the neighbourhood who remembered Maggie McLean and the fact that her son taught her to read some years after that letter was supposed to have been written," said Julian. "Uncle James confided in Beresford after Letta was murdered, and of course got politely called all sorts of a fool for having acted as he did."

I remembered that word 'madness' I had overheard and misinterpreted.

"He said he would have the whole matter investigated and then your father mentioned the coincidence of Laird having come from Glenairlie. He and Beresford decided that, as doctors were used to being let in on family secrets they might tell them enough to get his help and Dr. Robbie's advice."

Julian had got up and gone to the window, and now he turned and stood facing me with his back to the light.

"Silla, there's something else we had better talk about, now we have the opportunity," he said. "Us."

14

I KNEW that the opportunity I had been waiting for had come, and that I must tell him now that I couldn't marry him. I had wanted to tell him during our walk back to the lodge on the previous night. But he had been so kind. I had thought, too, that he might not take my words seriously in view of my shocked state.

"Julian," I began.

But he started to speak at the same time, and what he said was so surprising that I had to listen.

"Do you love me well enough to settle down with me in another country?" he asked gravely.

"What on earth do you mean?" I said. "What other country?"

He frowned. "The United States, of course. I've got the chance now of taking complete charge of the American side of the business, and I want to do it. I like the idea of living over there, too. How do you feel about it?"

"But Westings! My father!" I exclaimed.

"I have an idea your father will marry Miss Peach," he said. "Mother thought he was going to do before all this trouble started, you know. And we can pop over quite frequently. I suppose we'll inherit the old house one day. Of course I hope it won't be for a long time yet. When the day does come then we'll have to keep two homes going, one on either side of the Atlantic. I shall open the place to the public when I own it. After all, it's quite a museum. The visitors' half-crowns will help pay for the upkeep."

I stared at him, while my neat house of cards, which I had thought of gently taking down, collapsed in a jumbled heap.

"All right," he said in a different tone. "You don't love me well enough to live abroad with me. In fact, you don't love me well enough to marry me at all, do you, Silla?" His tone was sad rather than reproachful and I felt remorse.

"I — I'm very fond of you, Julian," I faltered.

"Oh, fond! You're very fond of Angelique and Jessup and the dogs," he said with a wry little laugh.

"You don't want me then?" I said, and I couldn't help it if there was a note of hope in my voice.

"Yes," he said abruptly, "I want you all right. But not on any terms. I might have put up with coming third to your father and Westings, but when you're obviously crazy about another man — "

"Julian!" I exclaimed.

"I mean Laird, of course," he said. "And there's no need to pretend."

"How did you know?" I asked feebly.

"It's been quite obvious," he told me shatteringly.

"The way you look at him, the way you say his name, the way you react when other people mention him. There have been times when I have wanted to rush off and punch him on the nose."

"I'm sorry, Julian," I said. But I wasn't. I was suddenly wildly elated. "At first I thought it was just a kind of infatuation," I explained.

"But it isn't?" said Julian.

I shook my head. "No. I think it's the real thing."

"Well, he's obviously mad about you," said my cousin gloomily.

"Oh Julian, do you really think so?" I said, trying not to sound too delighted.

"Yes, damn him!" said Julian. "Oh well, he'll make a good husband — solid as a rock. And he's booked for Harley Street some day, according to Robbie's friend the heart specialist. You know why he's vegetating down here, I suppose."

"No," I said breathlessly. "Why?"

"Well, Robbie told us last night that Laird had had a dose of rheumatic fever and it had pulled him down rather, without doing him any permanent damage, so he was ordered to take things quietly for six months. Robbie has kept dark about it because he says people don't like to think their doctors are subject to the same physical weakness they are, let alone moral. The six months are almost up now, so he'll soon be going back."

This filled me with a terrible sense of urgency. I wished Julian would go so that I could leap out of bed and rush to find Alan. But one thing was troubling me.

"Do you think Daddy will be terribly disappointed that I'm not going to marry you?" I asked anxiously.

Julian shrugged. "He'll get over it," he said. "To hell with Uncle James's disappointment, anyway. What about my disappointment?"

"You'll get over it too, darling," I said soothingly.

(He has, of course, and is happier with his vivacious American wife than he would ever have been with me.)

"There's one thing you'll have to put up with if you marry Laird," he added. "He has no sense of humour, poor chap!"

"Oh Julian, he has," I cried loyally, but I had some misgivings.

Of course I didn't rush off to find Alan right away, though I fretted inwardly at having to go about things tactfully, especially when I remembered that pretty sophisticated nurse and the fact that he thought I was all set to marry my cousin. In the end I phoned Woodside and asked Dr. Robbie if I could come to tea and if he would insure Alan's being present.

"I want to thank him properly for saving my life," I explained.

"Saving life is a doctor's privilege," said Dr. Robbie.

"Not quite in the same way Alan saved mine," I said warmly.

"All right, my dear," said the old doctor. "I'll see that he's there, and if a call comes for one of us at teatime, I'll take it." He gave a soft chuckle. "I might even invent one," he whispered.

He did too, bless him, and left Alan and me *tête-à-tête* across the silver teapot and Mrs. Budge's feathery sponge and golden brown scones.

"Alan," I faltered, "I — I don't know what to say to you — to thank you for saving me." My knees felt suddenly weak and I really was, for the moment, quite tongue-tied.

He frowned slightly and helped himself to a scone.

"It was Price's profession that saved you," he said. "Being an actor, he just had to make a dramatic scene in which he could star, instead of shooting you right away. It gave me time to get to the lodge." He took a bite of the scone.

"But you might have been badly hurt," I said.

He looked surprised. "I? Badly hurt?" he said. "*He* was the one in danger. When I saw your face I wanted to kill him." His eyes flashed at the memory.

I was secretly deeply thrilled, and disappointed to see him pull himself up and become suddenly wooden. He looked down at the bitten scone on his plate, then stood up. "If you'll excuse me — " he said austerely.

"Oh, I hope you're not going yet," I said, getting up also. "I was just about to tell you a piece of news that will soon be all over the village."

"Your marriage?" he said, as if the words tasted unpleasant.

"Quite the opposite," I said, smiling, though my heart was thumping away madly. "Julian and I have decided not to go through with it. He thinks I'm in love with another man."

Alan drew in his breath sharply. "And — are you?" he asked, staring at me piercingly.

"Yes," I said. " So much so that I'd even go and work in a Glasgow slum for him."

His face broke into a smile that was wonderful to see. "Havers woman!" he cried. "You in a Glasgow slum! You're going to be fully occupied with some bairns of your own to look after and a doctor's house to keep."

We both laughed crazily. Then I was in his arms, and it was far far better than that evening in the garden at Westings.

Later I said tenderly: "I shall never forget how you believed in my innocence when Julian really half-believed I'd drowned Letta. Why did you, my darling?"

"Well, it was all quite logical," he told me solemnly, but a twinkle came into his bright eyes. "I knew that I couldn't possibly be in love with a murderess and I *was* in love with you, therefore you *must* be innocent."

"Oh Alan!" I cried, delighted. "I knew you had a sense of humour somewhere."

"Well, of course," he said, amazed. "I just keep it for special occasions." And he showed me again how special this occasion was.

He had another surprise for me. He

was not so poor as I had imagined. There had been a legacy from a thrifty old godmother who had much approved of his taking up medicine. That, with my own small inheritance enabled us to marry quite soon, just in time for it still to be possible to have a marquee on the lawn at Westings before the Autumn was too far advanced.

Alan was right about the bairns and the doctor's house, but I find time in a very busy life to go down to Westings fairly often, where dear Mary makes as much of my baby daughter as she does of her beloved cats, and my father is as proud of his grandson as if his surname had been D'alquen and he was one day to inherit Westings.

Adrian Price is serving a life-sentence in one of Her Majesty's prisons. The great cedar still casts its shadow, but the ghost of poor William seems to have been laid.

A FOOT IN THE GRAVE
Bruce Marshall

About to be imprisoned and tortured in Buenos Aires, John Smith escapes, only to become involved in an aeroplane hijacking.

DEAD TROUBLE
Martin Carroll

Trespassing brought Jennifer Denning more than she bargained for. She was totally unprepared for the violence which was to lie in her path.

HOURS TO KILL
Ursula Curtiss

Margaret went to New Mexico to look after her sick sister's rented house and felt a sharp edge of fear when the absent landlady arrived.

THE DEATH OF ABBE DIDIER
Richard Grayson

Inspector Gautier of the Sûreté investigates three crimes which are strangely connected.

NIGHTMARE TIME
Hugh Pentecost

Have the missing major and his wife met with foul play somewhere in the Beaumont Hotel, or is their disappearance a carefully planned step in an act of treason?

BLOOD WILL OUT
Margaret Carr

Why was the manor house so oddly familiar to Elinor Howard? Who would have guessed that a Sunday School outing could lead to murder?

THE DRACULA MURDERS
Philip Daniels

The Horror Ball was interrupted by a spectral figure who warned the merrymakers they were tampering with the unknown.

THE LADIES
OF LAMBTON GREEN
Liza Shepherd

Why did murdered Robin Colquhoun's picture pose such a threat to the ladies of Lambton Green?

CARNABY
AND THE GAOLBREAKERS
Peter N. Walker

Detective Sergeant James Aloysius Carnaby-King is sent to prison as bait. When he joins in an escape he is thrown headfirst into a vicious murder hunt.

MUD IN HIS EYE
Gerald Hammond

The harbourmaster's body is found mangled beneath Major Smyle's yacht. What is the sinister significance of the illicit oysters?

THE SCAVENGERS
Bill Knox

Among the masses of struggling fish in the *Tecta's* nets was a larger, darker, ominously motionless form . . . the body of a skin diver.

DEATH IN ARCADY
Stella Phillips

Detective Inspector Matthew Furnival works unofficially with the local police when a brutal murder takes place in a caravan camp.

STORM CENTRE
Douglas Clark

Detective Chief Superintendent Masters, temporarily lecturing in a police staff college, finds there's more to the job than a few weeks relaxation in a rural setting.

THE MANUSCRIPT MURDERS
Roy Harley Lewis

Antiquarian bookseller Matthew Coll, acquires a rare 16th century manuscript. But when the Dutch professor who had discovered the journal is murdered, Coll begins to doubt its authenticity.

SHARENDEL
Margaret Carr

Ruth didn't want all that money. And she didn't want Aunt Cass to die. But at Sharendel things looked different. She began to wonder if she had a split personality.

MURDER TO BURN
Laurie Mantell

Sergeants Steven Arrow and Lance Brendon, of the New Zealand police force, come upon a woman's body in the water. When the dead woman is identified they begin to realise that they are investigating a complex fraud.

YOU CAN HELP ME
Maisie Birmingham

Whilst running the Citizens' Advice Bureau, Kate Weatherley is attacked with no apparent motive. Then the body of one of her clients is found in her room.

DAGGERS DRAWN
Margaret Carr

Stacey Manston was the kind of girl who could take most things in her stride, but three murders were something different . . .

THE MONTMARTRE MURDERS
Richard Grayson

Inspector Gautier of Sûreté investigates the disappearance of artist Théo, the heir to a fortune.

GRIZZLY TRAIL
Gwen Moffat

Miss Pink, alone in the Rockies, helps in a search for missing hikers, solves two cruel murders and has the most terrifying experience of her life when she meets a grizzly bear!

BLINDMAN'S BLUFF
Margaret Carr

Kate Deverill had considered suicide. It was one way out — and preferable to being murdered.